Zeynep Guvenc

HOME
LESS

Home-less

Copyright © 2016 Zeynep Guvenc

All rights reserved. No part of this publication may be reproduced, stored in a retrieval system or transmitted in any form or by any means, electronic, mechanical, photocopying, recording or otherwise, without the prior written permission of the author. The information, views, opinions and visuals expressed in this publication are solely those of the author. The author disclaim any direct or indirect liabilities or warranties arising from the use of information contained in this book. The reader should seek the advice of a competent professional where appropriate.

ISBN-13 978-1530886203 (CreateSpace-Assigned)
ISBN-10 1530886201

FIRST SCENE

Johnson stopped at the red light and began tottering in circles. He was turning around a pole, trying not to lose his balance and fall, so he looked like he was ice-skating. His head dropped in front of him, his hands were level with his waist. Sharp cold was entering through the many holes in his old jacket.

He was drunk. Gathering his beer bottles into a trolley, he pushed his home as if he was a turtle. The only difference between him and a turtle was his shelter was in his hands, not on his back. The lights turned green again. He hair was shaggy, his already black face even blacker because of the dirt. He always slept in front of an auto-mechanics'; there were paint stains on his temple.

He kept waiting at the red-light—unwillingly. The light turned green; he didn't go across the street. The light turned red again. It was 3 a.m., the streets were quiet, the sidewalks deserted.

The cars now began honking for him to cross the street. Johnson was playing with them. He grabbed his trolley firmly and pushed it back and forth. With every shake the bottles smashed together, sounding as if they were breaking. This possibility amused him.

He took a half hamburger from the garbage near the lights. "Somebody left this for me," he said, laughing. The hamburger had ants on it, but he didn't mind; he wrapped it and put it in a discolored patched blue sweater he had picked up from a friend.

He pushed the trolley rapidly right to the center of the road.

"Move on," yelled a young driver.

Johnson gave him the finger, said, "I'm not ready," and walked in the opposite direction. His wheeled house lost balance, glass smashing. First he crashed to the sidewalk then fall on the grass. Half of the bottles were broken.

Johnson turned his back on the trolley. "It is not my only house anyway," he said. The streets were his home; the trolley had nothing to do with his loneliness.

Now he was laughing. When things were at their most painful, the sound he made was somewhere between laughing and crying. He was emotionless and all alone. He wanted to throw up, but he gulped the nausea down—unsuccessfully. He spat randomly on the road and scraped his feet. He was expecting to feel the ground soft and slippery, instead he felt something crunchy. A piece of white paper stuck to his black sneakers.

He wanted to write something. He insisted on writing. He wanted to share his homesickness and loneliness, but had no pen. He was tired of walking, but he was close to the center. His homeless friends gathered in front of the park; he planned to ask them for a pen. A pen was a loyal friend. In his cell in the garage, he was able to breathe through writing and the pen never betrayed him. It was only when he grabbed his dreams that he could leave that cell.

There were eight to ten people in front of a wall. Some of them were lying on the ground, others were chatting. Johnson slowly went closer to the quietest of them.

"Diane, do you have a pen?"

"What? What are you talking about? Go away!"

Johnson looked silently at the murderer whose sleep he had interrupted. Jay had just come out of prison; he wanted to live in his dreams so the only thing he did was sleep. He looked like a skeleton; he would have been dead already if not for the food his friends found on the street. He was so uptight that he could kill anyone who disturbed him.

Jay took a step and threw a punch at Johnson's face. Johnson landed on the street. When the police on patrol came by, everyone calmed down and hid away in their corners.

Johnson barely managed to convinced the police that he hadn't started the fight. He kept saying, "But I only…But I only…"

Eventually Diane told the police, "It was not his fault, sir," and that's how he escaped arrest.

Johnson's eyes were bloodshot with purple and red circles around them. His nose was bleeding and there were some scratches on one of his cheeks. Sometimes he wished he did not have a mirror. Whenever his he saw his face he felt sorry for himself. He always felt sorry for himself, but at least he only had to cope with one type of pain. Seeing the pain and feeling it was completely different, and both seeing and feeling hurt him twice as much.

Why do people do this to themselves, hurting themselves twice? he thought.

"Break all mirrors!" he said and threw a stone at his reflection. This stone cracked the mirror like a starburst, splitting his reflection into three people.

Johnson kept on thinking what he would write. The words came rapidly into his mind, one after another. He couldn't stop them and he quickly repeated them so as not to forget them. He kept touching his eye with his right hand; he had been punched hard and it hurt. He stood up, limping toward the wing mirror of a red car parked on the sidewalk. Leaning into the mirror, he saw his face again.

"Go to hell, Jay," he said through gritted teeth. "Die, you bag of bones". The car alarm went off, startling Johnson and he ran away quickly, out of breath, holding his chest with his left hand. He was afraid of running, for running meant he was escaping from something. In his nightmares, he was always running away from someone, and he would wake up in a sweat just before that someone caught him.

Now he was hiding behind a bank in a churchyard and his heartbeat got even quicker when he heard the police sirens. A sharp ray of light shone in his eye: a torch, pointing at his face. A priest in long black robes lowered his head and said, "Hey, stranger, come with me," in a low voice, as if he was trying not to scare a small animal.

The priest was so confident Johnson would follow that he turned his back to him and walked away. Looking all around the garden carefully, Johnson had already made his plan just before the priest had arrived. Now, he jumped from the gap between the walls that he'd had in his sights. The priest kept his mouth shut. Johnson knew that the priest would give him some food, and the priest knew he was hiding from the police. Two strangers had touched each other's lives in the dead of night, yet the priest's willingness to do him a favor stuck in Johnson's throat.

Johnson escaped from the hands of the police in the Market Street and now he was throwing up. Throwing up was crying out for him as his stomach was empty. He was throwing up his emptiness. How big was this emptiness; how homeless; how roofless?

He wanted to boil up the words in his mind and drink them. It was dark, cold and there were no newspapers. Newspapers were thin, but he could pretend they were a quilt. Instead he made the words into a quilt and slept in a corner. The words warmed him up, or was he deceiving himself? He needed to be deceived. He felt safe then; he would sleep. He had got rid of the trolley, but he couldn't get rid of himself and his damn corpse so easily.

FIRST SCENE

"You're all dead, all corpses I see," he said in a low voice. Then his voice got a little higher; he cleared his throat a couple of times and expectorated. "Hey, there are others in your place now. You were not here a hundred years ago and will not be here in a hundred years time. Who were you then? Who will you be?"

He closed his mouth and bit his finger, hurting himself so much that he painted his hand red.

★

Lara stood under the plate 'The Embarcadero'. She raised her head and said enthusiastically, "Oh yes, I remember this. Embarcadero comes from the Spanish word *embarcar*, which means embark in English—namely to depart, to start a journey. Now we are starting a journey, we will see what it will bring to our lives!"

She raised her shoulders, then lowered them as if waiting for applause.

Sadaf asked in surprise, "How come you know all this, Lara?"

"I did a little research before I came to San Francisco."

"The name of the street and its origins?" Meltem asked.

"Yes, I exaggerated a little. Just curiosity." She shrugged her shoulders again.

Cihan said, "You linked nicely to the name of the film," and nodded his head in admiration.

Cihan, Meltem, Lara and Sadaf entered the cinema in Embarcadero Street. The commercial was over and the movie *Life* had started. The youngsters asked an elderly couple to help them find their seats on the row. The tall thin woman made a face as if to say "You should have come earlier"; the man, on the other hand, smiled at them, apologizing for her, got to his feet and showed them to their places one by one.

Lara started throwing popcorn into her mouth by handful. When Cihan reached his hand into the box, some of the popcorn fell onto Lara's lap.

Meltem told Cihan, "You can take some of my popcorn," but Cihan silenced his sister.

"This way is easier."

Four pairs of eyes locked on the screen as the scenes began passing one by one—1, 2, 3, 4, 5, 6...

★

The night seemed like it had got a lot colder. There was no one in sight except a few homeless under the streetlights.

Meltem took Cihan by the arm and said, "Slow down, bro." She was jealous of her brother paying attention to the two other girls and pulled him to her side.

"What's up, Meltem? You have never called me bro before. Have you just realized that I'm your brother?"

"Don't make fun of me, I'm just scared!" said Meltem, curling her lips like a little child.

"You have lived in San Francisco for many years and you are still not used to these homeless people? Don't be afraid, they won't eat you. Let's move!"

Cihan pressed his arm muscles with his right hand, being a little bit macho The youngsters looked away from the homeless man; he was a blur person, and ignoring him was the best.

"He'll probably want money, that's the trouble," said Cihan, adding in a worried voice, "Girls, be quick!"

Sadaf asked, "Lara, did you see the guy's eyes?"

"Nope!" answered Lara lightly.

FIRST SCENE

"Oh my God, they look unreal, Lara. Look, big blue eyes on a black face!"

"What's wrong with that?"

"It's interesting. Well, I am surprised. I have never seen a blue-eyed African-American before."

*

Johnson slowly moved nearer and stopped in front of a brown-haired hazel-eyed woman in a mustard colored jacket.

"Pretty lady," he said, bowing his head. Putting his hand on his heart, he waited for thanks while grinning. Johnson loved his blue eyes on his black face: they were so beautiful and deep like an ocean. His friends called him night-sea, and sometimes they were even afraid to look at him. The sea was even scarier at night.

Lara didn't know what to do when she heard the homeless man give her a compliment. She opened her big eyes even wider—almost half of her face was eye now—threw the popcorn on the ground and began walking quicker. Johnson stood where he was and threw his unwashed braid back.

"What about me, nice lady?" To be liked was a basic human need. Maybe he would turn into a prince like in the fairy-tale. No, he was filth. Why did the truth have to attack his brain so fast? Why slap his dirtiness into his face?

*

Lara ran on her high heels without looking back, her heart in her mouth. When she had bought her shoes from Forever 21 she had wondered whether she would be able to walk in them without falling. Now she was running in them. Life was strange.

"Where did you park the damn car Cihan? Open that damn door quick!" she said, swinging from right to left. Cihan didn't know whether she was cold or needed to pee. He half-opened his mouth, raised his eyebrows and looked her as if to say *Are you talking to me?*

Then, shaking the car keys in Lara's face, he said, "Here is just like Istanbul, young lady. We have a lot of parking problems. If you had spent a little less time in front of the mirror, we could have parked the car nearer."

★

Meltem had to count sheep to sleep. Cihan had put his earphones in; 'Far From Heaven' was playing and his thin pink lips were moving.

Lara regarded the sky in her mind without fear for the first time. There were too many stars in her heart. She delved a little more to see the truth; to comprehend the difference between looking out the window and looking at the window. Lara opened all her windows and cleared her soul, peace brewing in her heart. She took a deep breath, like inhaling the scent of fresh soil. When she smelled her own scent, the nose of her heart ached. She looked out the window, but the window did not look back, just like the far away man she loved.

Sadaf had finally realized that night she had no place in Cihan's heart. It had been pointless for her to beg Lara to go to the cinema with them. Sadaf was no more than a guest; Lara lived in the heart of the man Sadaf loved. Sleeping in the same house as him gave her a great thrill of excitement, even if it did not mean anything to him. Now Cihan was in the room next to hers, maybe in his bed. Being homeless in a home was like that; she was like the man they had seen on the street. She was unprotected at night. The whole world was watching her, looking up, and there was no roof. Being so close to him felt like lying near the fire; she had worked up a sweat in a moment. Throwing the quilt off and leaning her elbows on the bed, she looked up.

"Hey, Lara, are you sleeping?" she asked, shaking her hair from her eyes.

"I'm not," Lara said calmly, although she sounded tired. She didn't turn her head to Sadaf; her eyes were locked on the ceiling.

"Do you know what I am thinking? Cihan likes you," said Sadaf. This time she lifted all her hair and pushed it back onto her shoulders.

Lara gave a huff and sat up from her pillow, her face falling. "I've already told you that I don't care, Sadaf. Take Cihan, he is yours,"

"And yours, Lara, is in Turkey, while you're still..."

Sadaf regretted the words the moment she had said them. She lowered herself into her bed; she did not know where to hide from her shyness and escape from her words.

Lara gritted her teeth. Shaking her finger at Sadaf, she said, "Don't you ever say 'still' to me like the others!" then turned over.

Her back to Sadaf, Lara pulled the quilt over her head and said harshly, "Good night!" Only a part of Lara's back was covered, and Sadaf couldn't help looking at the wave of her hair on the pillow. Lara was beautiful, and she was Turkish. On the other hand, Sadaf was Pakistani. Of course Cihan would choose Lara, but the problem was Lara didn't want to be on the pedestal on which Cihan put her.

"I'm sorry, Lara, I didn't mean to hurt you, but when we were at the cinema I saw how Cihan looked at you."

Her words stuck in her throat with Lara's reply.

"I want to sleep, please!"

"Okay, all right. Good night!" said Sadaf and sank into the bed again. She wanted the feelings inside her to sink as well, but when pushed away they kept returning, swimming around her heart waters. Sadaf was in the home of her love, but outside of his heart so what was the point being near him? There was only a wall separating them. Would Cihan come to her if he knew her heart was beating for him? What would happen even if he did?

★

Nuray was examining herself in the mirror while brushing her teeth in the bathroom with the green tiles. Either she had gained weight again or this mirror always made her look fat. Maybe it was the mirror that had gained weight, not her.

Şahin took off his glasses and rubbed his eyes. Then he continued to write.

"Won't you get some sleep, Şahin?" asked his wife for the third time. He ignored her.

When Nuray asked for a fourth time, he said, "Don't wait for me. Go to bed, please, I have some more things to do."

Still looking at the mirror, Nuray had expected that answer. She walked without looking back, scuffing her feet, wearing her woolen snowman Walgreens slippers. They were keeping her feet warm, but her heart was frozen. She was becoming a snowwoman herself.

In her bedroom, dashing away her tears silently, she started melting the snow.

★

Cihan gave up on sleep and opened his laptop. His phone was on mute; he had forgotten to look at it after he'd left the cinema.

He saw *one new message* on the screen:

Cihan, don't want to have to call my parents. Bro, look at your damn phone.

When Cihan called Edom, it was 2.34 a.m. There were noises on the other end of the phone.

"Ha-alo a-l-o," said Edom, then there was silence again.

Cihan asked, "Where are you, Edi? Call a taxi. Why are you calling me?"

"I can't call a taxi, I have no money."

"Come on!"

"Really, I have none. I came here with a friend. He is now fast asleep."

"Don't you have your card? You can pay when you get back home. Okay, don't cry. I will come and pick you up. Where are you?" Cihan coughed.

"I'm at San Jose, waiting for you. There is no place to sleep. Everybody already picked all the places. You'll..."

Edom sounded drunk and Cihan was only able to understand him after he'd repeated his words couple of times.

"Okay, I'm on my way," said Cihan and hung up.

*

Cihan occasionally glanced at Edom's face, then he looked again at the road. Edom was lying on the seat like a flour sack, his white jersey and blue skinny jeans matching his blond hair and dark blue eyes. Whenever Edom tried to put his head on Cihan's shoulders, Cihan shrugged him off. Then Edom would shake his head, asking, "What?"

"Stop doing that. Can't you see I am driving?"

"Okay, you coward. Drive, nothing will happen," said Edom smiling, then he went back to sleep.

Cihan took out a bottle of water and sprinkled some on Edom's face when they stopped at the lights. Startled, Edom opened his eyes wide.

"What the hell are you doing?"

"Waking you up. You can't go home like this. You say your mom gets upset every time you drink too much, but you continue to do it."

"Don't give me a sermon, just take me home. I have a terrible headache." Edom put his arm on the window and opened it a little. Closing his eyes and breathing in the air, he said, "The breeze is so nice!"

"The breeze? Are you mad? The wind is so damn cold, we're gonna freeze. Close that window, I don't want to get cold."

"Why didn't you come to the party?" asked Edom, suddenly serious. He was looking out of the window, silent and clearheaded.

"I already told you that I would be at the movies with the girls, remember?"

Edom bit his lip and thought what to say next. "How is Lara?"

Cihan said, "Well, very well," then turned the volume up. 'Losing My Religion' was on the radio and Cihan sang along, losing himself in the song. Edom put his palms together and rubbed his fingers.

"I guess I'm losing mine too," he mumbled.

"What did you say? Didn't hear," said Cihan, turning the volume down but still singing: "*It was just a dream, just a dream...*"

"I'm losing my faith, Cihan," Edom said with his eyes full of tears. He turned his head, seeming like he was looking at a parade on the window, deep in his thoughts. How could one person change that fast? It was hard to believe the person who had been slumped like a bag five minutes before was the same one saying these wise words now.

Cihan asked, "What do you mean by faith?"

"I don't have faith in love anymore," said Edom, lifting his small pointed nose with his fingers. Cihan lowered his head toward him as the music was too loud.

"You will fall in love," he said, laughing. "Who could resist someone as handsome as you anyway?"

Edom said, "That person can," and leaned his head back. "Whatever, forget it!"

"Take a shower and get a good rest! Call me when you feel better, we're going to train for the marathon, okay?"

The car stopped in front of one of the big white mansions on Broadway Street. Cihan got out of the car, opened Edom's door and threw his arm around his neck, dragging him to the steps. When they were finally at the door, Cihan said, "I hope you've got your keys." His attention was caught by something on the door. "What is this small fancy thing?"

"Well, it is a mezuzah," answered Edom, "Haven't you seen it before?"

"No, never noticed it before. What does mezuzah mean?"

"Rannan is Jewish, Cihan, have you forgotten? Mezuzah is a verse from the Torah that Jews put on their doors."

"For God's protection? What is written inside?"

"You won't understand, what is the point of telling you?"

"I'll get it if you tell me!"

"*Barukh ata Adonai Eloheinu Melekh ha-olam, asher kidshanu b'mitzvotav v'tzivanu likbo-a mezuza.*"

"Well of course not in Hebrew, Edi, tell me in English!"

"Blessed are You, Lord our God, King of the Universe, who sanctified us with His mitzvoth, and commanded us to affix a mezuzah."

Cihan was about to open the door but it opened itself. It was Maya, the housekeeper. She looked at them with sleepy eyes and whispered, "Where have you been, young sir? Your mother was worried about you."

Edom hushed her and turned to wave at Cihan. The big white door closed in Cihan's face. Maya was a grumpy lady.

*

The difference between night and day was the same as the difference between hot and cold for Johnson. There was no night for him, but cold. The name of the day was 'Hot'. Now, Johnson was as cold as the face of death. He was lying on the street with a broken bottle in his hand. There was blood on the bottle. Johnson had wanted to get warm when the youngsters had left so he'd cut his wrists.

He thought it was day, but this warmness was different indeed. He was bleeding; his heart stopped.

He had no idea what color the light was. His eyes closed. His eyes opened.

And the sun rose for someone...

*

Johnson slept until nine at the train station. He couldn't believe he was able to sleep in such a noisy place. Every other night was a new adventure. He stood up, shook his covers off and walked to Van Ness. He found some cardboard, one of the many cardboard boxes the homeless hid behind the garbage bin, stopped at the traffic lights and sat on the sidewalk, a sad and lifeless look on his face. It was the look of one who had nothing to lose, and it was the only look that triggered people's moral compass, so he thought it was the best look to have.

Johnson watched the cars waiting for the lights to turn green. Different sizes, colors and brands, so many cars and trucks slowing and stopping on the street. He felt important for a moment; he thought the cars were stopping not for the lights, but for him. He imagined they did not stop to give him money but signs, then laughed at himself for imagining that.

Johnson got up and pulled up his pants. He tightened a white rope around his waist, but they never felt comfortable. Two days ago, he had stolen these brown pants from a dryer in a launderette. He didn't know whose pants they were, but they were at least two sizes too big for him. As a final solution he rolled the pants up a couple of times, but now they were too short for him. He looked ridiculous, he was sure, but his whole life was tragicomic. He was a thirty-year-old man with no home, no job—nothing at all.

Johnson was shaking a plastic cup at the drivers. He was ashamed to be asking for money, but it was even more shaming for them not to give him any when they could. He had such anger toward money.

The window of a white Mercedes opened and Johnson ran towards it. He said, "God bless you," and smiled.

An obese white American man with thinning hair put three quarters in the cup. The coins tinkled.

Johnson was pissed off as he had run to get the money as the lights turned green and all he got was three quarters. He left the cup under the traffic lights and held his *Homeless, I need money* sign up.

The driver approaching might give me some money, he thought. In the new white BMW there was an Asian woman. She looked at the homeless man as if he was not there, her eyes hidden behind her sunglasses. Although paying attention to him, she wanted to be seen as if she were not, but her hands shook for a moment. The homeless man upset her, following all the other troubles in her day. She looked to her right, then her left, deciding to focus on the mirror, licking her lipstick a couple of times. She tied up her hair on the top of her head, pushing the forelocks out of her face. She looked at only herself and not at the man outside of the car. While not looking, she didn't realize she was actually concentrating on him.

Ashamed of what she had, she stepped furiously on the gas. The homeless man was left behind, but would be with her all the time. He would be with her at home, at her desk, on her chair, in her bathroom. Homelessness stuck to her all the time, and when what she wanted to leave behind was always with her, she hid from herself, even though she knew she would reach rock bottom before herself.

SECOND SCENE

The sunshine was dancing its afternoon crimson beams in San Francisco. The windows of the green house at 69 Turk Street were all open and Nuray could see the sunlight's farewell from where she was. Then she looked at the laundry, a big mountain she had put on the cream bed sheets. She was going to fold the items one by one. She was crying, the drops finding their way onto the violet towel right in front of her; she was sinking under the laundry. The clothes she wore got dirty, she washed them and dried them. It marked the days passing, one by one, making her stoop until she got into bed once more.

She decided to begin not at the top of the mountain but in the middle. She took what was at eye level first: her nude undershirt. The lace had ripped in the dryer. She pulled the fiber from the leaf pattern, wanting to pull off it, but she stopped. Then she took the split between her teeth and pulled it off in one go.

Irritated, Nuray put the underwear on her knees and pressed the garment as if she were doing the ironing. She felt her own hands on her neck, on her jugular vein, massaging it. With her finger, she touched her golden chain, following the ladybug on the tip. Her eyes stopped once her heart began to talk.

She took a little item of underwear, patterned with cars, and grasped it firmly. It was only the love of a child that could make her smile. It was as if Emir, her littlest child, had come into the room, sat on the top of the mountain and taken all her sorrow.

When she had finished folding the laundry her sorrow got even bigger. While she was putting it in the drawers, she also put her sorrows into the drawers of her heart. That's how she managed with her sorrow. She knew why her chest was burning. She had broken the mountain into pieces, into crumbs. She could not handle a mountain, but she could deal with the pieces in the drawers. She was able to put up with them one by one, but not all together.

Not a pile up, she thought.

She was always in an anxiety train, full of people reminding her of all the mistakes other people made. This train was followed by a homesickness train.

"I'm alone in this foreign land. My parents are not with me, I'm all alone." By excluding her family of four, she sat on the loneliness throne. She closed all the doors, locked them, refusing to be called or touched. The keys were hers and hers alone, and if she did not let herself out, she would be inside forever. This complicated situation made her challenge her inner circle, and her husband mostly. Why didn't he call, ask how she was? Was she his wife or a complete stranger? Was she a special person or an ordinary one?

She wasn't where she thought, because she thought herself to be nowhere. She put herself in a small cell, locked its doors and destroyed the keys. She squeezed herself in, her sorrows occupying more room than herself. At least they were in drawers that could be opened, but Nuray had locked herself in the room between death and life.

She wanted to walk away, but she would find no peace as she would be with herself all the time anyway. Wherever she went, she would find something to complain about, always wanting something else like a little child, giving herself no rest. She wanted to leave herself behind, leave the mountain of laundry behind, free herself from the drawers, her sorrow. It was good to collect her happiness, but collecting sorrow was not good. When it was a small pile it was easy to manage, but not when it became a mountain.

Life was sometimes an iron jacket. She couldn't move in it. Life went on, she was motionless. She was supposed to fall when she stopped, but she couldn't even do that. She just froze. She was pulled away from place and time. Kicking away the stool, she hanged herself, eyes bulging.

In her childhood, she'd had to hang out laundry to dry it, but now she could just put it in a dryer and it could easily turn into mountain. The wind would dry it, indeed, but now the wind would not because it became heavier when wet. She just couldn't carry it. She used to put laundry on her hipbone to carry it back in Konya. Now, the laundry dried in the green house at 69 Turk Street in San Francisco. The wind might be accused of not drying the laundry, but it was her sorrow that got it dirty.

It would be tomorrow again soon. The sorrow would get heavier; there would be more laundry with irremovable stains. The wind would complain to the clothesline and swear at it. Tomorrow would be today and today would turn into yesterday.

Nuray came to the bedroom door sniffing and opened it slowly. She tiptoed in. Şahin was snoring in his long-sleeved pajamas, holding onto the entire quilt as always. Nuray was wearing her white pajamas with pink flower patterns. She took off her gray velvet headband and hung it on the nightstand. She would have brushed her teeth after having had tea, but she didn't want to bother her husband again.

She took the light-green sateen quilt from between her husband's legs.

Şahin asked, "Are you here?" and turned his back. His eyes were closed. Nuray didn't answer him and lay down on the left side, immediately curling into the fetal position. When Şahin heard her sigh, he woke up and turned to her.

Şahin said, "I have seen Meltem's grades on the table. Such a disaster! We waste our money on her. I will talk to her tomorrow. She can't go on like that."

"You will," said Nuray, sniffing.

"What's wrong? Are you crying?"

"Nothing's wrong. Sleep well, Şahin," answered Nuray without turning her face to him.

"Well, something is wrong. You watch TV every night till late, and then you cry in bed. If TV programs make you cry, why do you keep watching them?"

Nuray had been caught out. She needed to pacify him.

"I weep with joy. The lovers came together, the father got out of the prison, and the mother got well. It was the final episode," said Nuray, puckering up her lips. She wanted to make him feel sorry for her, but Şahin reacted the opposite way and got angry.

"What a joy, the lovers got together! This only happens in the movies, not in real life. Tell me, who is really with their true love?"

Sleepiness had made him speak his unconscious mind: he was not with his love; his mind was still on someone else. Nuray was silent, but filled with sorrow she felt more like crying than ever.

"Do not watch that TV series again. I am serious!" said Şahin, shaking his finger at her. Nuray held her tongue. The reality of the TV series disappeared and now she was in her own fake world. Her marriage was fake. All of her story was fake.

THIRD SCENE

Mariana was looking out of the window of the bus. A strong wind was blowing through the street of San Francisco. Like a child who was angry with his mom, the wind was charging along the streets, screaming.

Mariana asked her teddy bear, "The wind kid is quite naughty, right, Bo?"

A man with blue eyes smiled at her from under his cap. Mariana did not know what to say, but even so she smiled back.

The man moved closer.

"Nice teddy bear. What is his name?"

It was not clear if the African-American in the baseball cap was talking to her. He was hugging a bus pole and looking out of the window, and Mariana had never seen someone who did not look in the same direction they were speaking. She was the only person with a teddy bear, though.

"Bo," she answered and turned to the window, shaking her two braids tied with grape hair ties.

Rebecca was writing a message to her boss while biting her lips.

I'm a little late. I'll be on my way right after dropping my daughter at school.

By the way, Mariana started a conversation with a stranger.

"That's cool. It is cold because of the wind. That's why I have been on the bus since morning."

"It's only nine, when did you get on the bus?"

"It was seven so I have been here for five hours."

"No, that's two hours."

"No, seven hours."

Mariana was silent. She didn't want to get even more confused.

"Shhh, Bo, be quiet! He must be very bad at math. Don't let him make us bad at math as well, okay?" she whispered into Bo's ears, then returned her attention to the stranger.

"It is not even a trip. You're going to all the same places over and over. That is ridiculous."

"Doesn't matter. I don't get cold in here, and it is very cold outside."

"Then stay at a shop or in the church. I think going around by bus is meaningless."

"It's none of your business, kiddo!"

Mariana held her nose first and then the small pink teddy bear's.

"He does smell bad, doesn't he."

Rebecca was startled by a sob. It was Mariana crying. She put her phone in her back pocket and quickly hugged her, asking what had happened. Whining, Mariana told her everything.

"We were playing. He said he can make Bo talk with the wind, so I gave Bo to him," pointing at the African-American guy, "but now he won't give him back."

"Excuse me, sir, could you please give Bo to my daughter?"

A voice inside Rebecca was saying: *Look, I still call you sir, I'm still polite*, as if the homeless did not deserve to be treated humanely.

The homeless man shrugged and continued looking out of the window. This time Rebecca stamped her feet with frustration.

"Please, sir, please!"

"Hahaha! This is my teddy bear. If you want to get him back, you should pay me!"

"How come?" said Rebecca. "We both know he is my daughter's. She was playing with him just now." Rebecca grasped Mariana and pulled her close.

"I know, but she gave him to me of her own accord."

"All right, but just for a while, not for you to keep. Moreover, toys are for children, not for adults," said Rebecca, softening her voice to try and persuade him. She didn't want to upset the homeless because she couldn't expect anything good from them. She knew she had to be careful.

"Look, sir, give him back. Otherwise…"

She shook her finger at him then stopped.

"Well? Otherwise what?" He laughed. "Will you call police for a teddy bear?"

"Mom, I want Bo," Mariana said, tugging her mother's light green jacket.

"Okay," said Rebecca and took five dollars from her purse, "take this. I will buy Bo from you."

Although the bus was crowded, everyone else was minding their own business. Nobody intended to interfere in what was happening. Rebecca didn't like this ridiculousness, but there was nothing else she could do. She would not go to the police for a teddy bear, as the homeless man already knew.

"We got into trouble again," said the homeless man to Bo, then added to Rebecca, "Can you leave, madam? The teddy bear is not five dollars, but much more expensive!"

He got off the bus in the blink of the eye, leaving both Rebecca and Mariana shocked, and waved the hand holding Bo.

"Thanks, young lady, it is the greatest present I have ever had!" he said and kissed the teddy bear.

Rebecca had to comfort Mariana who was crying heavily.

"It's okay, honey. We'll buy a new one."

"No, I want Bo. He is my best friend."

"If so, why did you give him to the homeless guy? I have told you not to speak the homeless people, even if they speak to you.

"But he spoke with the wind, and I…"

"Okay, all right. We are late for school. Let's get off and walk fast."

She wiped her daughter's tears. As Mariana ran to her class, both of her braids and her backpack jigged up and down and her lunchbox bumped on her leg.

Rebecca took a taxi from the front of the school.

"Dolphin Restaurant, please."

Passing Transamerica Pyramid, she looked at her roman numbered triangle watch with the black leather strap and thought about what to tell her boss.

When Rebecca entered Dolphin Restaurant it was half past ten. She was supposed to be early that day for the accounting control; the boss had scheduled a meeting at ten. Rebecca tied her hair up tightly to make her eyes slant, even though she had headache. She said hi to the janitor with Down's Syndrome then knocked on her boss's door.

"What do you mean by deficit? You know everything is on my computer," Chun-Sun was saying in a beguiling voice.

"Yes, everything is written down, but some of the orders did not reach the tables. The customers were still charged. Where is

THIRD SCENE

that money? Not in the safe. Who would take it? Seven thousand dollars disappeared in three weeks—how?"

Bald, mustached, short and thin, the man became a giant with his words. When he said to Chun-Sun, "You can leave now, Rebecca is next," her hands got cold. A few minutes ago she was only concerned about being late for work, but now she was worried she'd be accused of stealing money. She couldn't believe it.

"I have no connection to this situation, sir. You know, you'd better ask the waiters."

"Of course we've asked them. What they told us is that you need money these days. You cannot pay your rent. You have even asked for money from them, even though you got an advance last month. What happened? Doesn't the father of your child pay the rent?"

"Yes, Boss, but he told me he won't anymore, the son of a bitch"

"Excuse me?"

"Nothing, sir. Anyway, I don't want to talk about my private issues. It's true that I have financial difficulties at the moment; but that doesn't mean I've stolen. I'm innocent."

"Even if that's true, we can't work with you anymore. You must leave."

"But, sir, what about my twenty-day pay?"

"No, you've already cost me a lot of money. I can't give you more."

"But that's my money!"

"Young lady, you'd better leave the room immediately or I'll call the police." And he slammed his fist on the table and stood up. He only came up to Rebecca's shoulders, but he was scary enough.

Rebecca left the room and went to the bathroom. She was about to cry but held herself. She washed her face, then dried it on the cheap paper towels.

The man behind the desk said, "You can't open your computer anymore. Take your belongings and leave please!"

Rebecca couldn't believe what she was going through. She had lost everything because of slander. She remembered how Mariana had given her the pencils with bunnies on. "Please, Mom, write with these and remember me!" she had said when she'd visited her at the restaurant. Her daughter had always been with her in that room. In fact, she was always with her in all of the rooms she had ever been in.

★

Rebecca wasn't prepared to leave her home; she had nowhere to go. Could one pack up without knowing where to go? The homeless man who had stolen Bo came into her mind. She made a sour face, then gulped. Now Rebecca was homeless as well, but she couldn't confess it to Mariana.

She was hardly able to hold back her tears. She kept turning her eyes away from Mariana. Rebecca put on her brown cashmere coat, pulled her hair into a bun and put it inside her mustard knitted hat. It had been a long time since she had gone out without makeup.

Rebecca dressed Mariana in her kitty anorak, adjusted her collar and put yellow gloves on her little hands. Having a final gaze around her home, she took her case and opened the door, noticing an envelope. She bent to pick it up, it but it tore in half. This upset her: her name was split in two, her life broken into pieces. The name of the person without a home was ripped in half. She became Reb from that moment on.

Then she looked at who the letter had come from. "It's too late, now," she said. As a final solution, she had asked for help from her father in Mexico. Reb did not even look at what was inside the envelope. She locked it inside the house.

THIRD SCENE

"Maybe," she said, "tomorrow will be different. But tomorrow will never come. Every day becomes today eventually."

On the corner, there was a man . Mariana asked, "Mom, this man doesn't have home?"

"I guess not. Let's walk faster!" She pulled Mariana beside.

"Mom, is he homeless just like us?"

"No, Mariana. How do you come up with these ideas?"

"I feel so sorry for the homeless man, Mom. Poor them. Luckily we are not like them."

"Yes, luckily."

Islands

The human body is made up of about 60% of water. A human should know how to swim so as not to drown in their own soul. Whenever tired, it is better for one to go to the islands in one's soul and rest. Which island one chooses depends on one's mood. If one is content, their soul will be on Angel Island. One who is kind will move to Treasure Island to pick up their presents. On these islands, time is frozen and peaceful. One smiles in every condition. In the darkest times, every light is on. These islands in one's inner world are heaven on earth.

When a person has regrets or a guilty conscience, their soul will travel to prison on Alcatraz Island. It is sunny everywhere else, but over their heads black clouds appear. Their faces are sullen and they have forgotten how to smile. Whoever comes to this island falls into the dungeon, even if they live in a palace. Their conscience bothers them all the time.

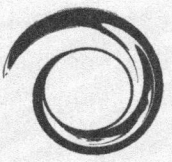

Treasure Island: The Machine of States

Two dreams were moving along like trains, then they got separated and went on different paths. Finally they found each other in the sky. Neither of them liked each other. If they had met in a different time, they would have liked each other, but the conditions were not under their control. The state of death became reality in a living being. The state of death was like a silk dress: smooth and soft, cool, but it could easily fall to the ground.

Meltem didn't like the dreams she was in that day. She felt like she had gone to a wedding wearing sportswear, or to play sport wearing a nightdress. She was feeling irritated, as if a man had put his arm on her shoulder without asking or someone she didn't know had called her deary. She didn't want anybody to hug her or call her dear. How improper was that?

This state was not good for her, but she always seemed to be in it. She thought she would explode whenever she breathed. She was not angry at the state she was in, but the road she had to travel while in that state.

Life was a change of state machine. A human entered the machine and changed their states. Particles were sent to enlighten the body. The machine of life was preparing to turn a dark world into a light one.

As a human, Meltem wore her state like a dress. Her face and body were the same; the only thing changing was the state she was in. The place, the time, the relationships could be the same, but when the state changed the sky would become black and yellow or the sun would become blue. No matter what you said, the result was different than your expectation. The language of the state was strange, yet the last word was its.

When a person was in one state, they wouldn't behave as they would in another. All they knew was the state they were in.

Meltem was in another time's state. All the years that had passed formed an identity for her. She didn't show anyone, but watched herself in the mirror. When she looked she saw a weary face, and she was bored of that. She was a mannequin for the strange states she was in, unable to stop herself.

When she thought she had finally stopped, she was actually in the train of regrets.

FOURTH SCENE

Meltem was leaning against the gray wall beside the showcase where the pumpkins with orange lights were. She was swaying on her feet, smiling occasionally and pretending to have fun. But she couldn't keep the forced smiles going much longer. She was unhappy at this Halloween party.

She was wearing a long white dress, a pair of wings and a headband like a halo. To give some curl to her hair she had slept with rollers in the night before. Now the curls had lost their form, which was one of the reasons she was in a bad mood. Efforts to be pretty always made her tired.

The idea of wearing the angel costume had been her mom's. She had kept saying, "My daughter can't be a witch. She is a real angel!" It was her mom who had persuaded her that she would be pretty, but Meltem did not like her appearance. She was dark and thin and looked as if she would split in half at the waist because the dress made her legs look even thinner.

Everyone at the house party was strange their own way that night. As if the sound of the electric guitar was not enough, the class rebel, Sun, was hitting the piano keys wildly. He was the center of attention in his pirate costume, and the noise of the crowd was getting louder.

Meltem pretended to drink from her cup, but actually she was trying to keep up with her friends. Spiderman and Catwoman were pulling each other's hair. Tom in a Dracula costume and Betie in a Sleeping Beauty costume were dancing on the table. Nicole was giving them a black look.

Nicole seemed to have come straight out of a witch movie with her long black deep-slitted dress, witch hat, decayed teeth and black circles around her eyes. She was plump with freckles on her white skin. Nobody would call Nicole beautiful at first sight, but she had an innocent look. That night she straightened her curly hair, even though Meltem had insisted she shouldn't.

Meltem asked Nicole, "Why did you want to be a witch?"

"Because I want to be the ugliest, the worst person there. I only have one night to be a bad woman, and I don't need to explain myself as I am a wicked witch."

Meltem couldn't relate being ugly and bad to being free. She avoided even thinking about the appeal of being a bad woman.

Nicole waved a packet of chips and asked Meltem, "Do you want any?"

"No." Meltem was bored to death; all she wanted was for this craziness to end so she could leave. Her father was out of town, otherwise she wouldn't have been able to come to the party. If it hadn't been for her mother, her second father, namely her brother, wouldn't have let her either.

"Leave her alone, Cihan," her mother had told him. "Let her have fun with her friends." Yet she felt it wasn't worth it. The party at number 27 was dull. Meltem was introvert and shy. Her friend Nicole had to drag her everywhere. If not, Meltem would spend all her time, apart from school time, at home. Her life was plain just like her—thin, plain, ordinary.

Meltem pulled Nicole's hair.

"Touching the witch's hat is bad luck, Angel. Stop it," said Nicole, still gazing at Tom and Betie.

Dracula Tom took Sleeping Beauty inside his cape."

Nicole covered her face.

"Did you know that?"

"Know what?"

"That Betie and Tom are together?"

"No, there is nothing between them." Nicole puckered her lips and admired her black nail polish.

"How do you know that?"

"Betie told me."

"She told you what?"

"Tom and she are friends with benefits."

"What?"

"You know nothing. They are only together in a sexual way, nothing romantic. Get it?"

"Like animals then?"

"Don't be ridiculous!"

"You said no emotions. Well, animals have no emotions. What have they done then, gone to the doctor to remove their ability to love? Anyway, you are still in love with Tom, that's what I don't get."

"You can't, Melo, you are an angel. Don't confuse your little brain."

"Go to hell!" said Meltem. Putting her cup on the table in a huff, she walked toward the piano.

"Look, Pirate Sun, move to another ship. You have given me headache, stop it!"

Sun pulled her arm and made her sit on his lap. Meltem screamed and stood up immediately. The music stopped and everyone began laughing at them.

"Oh, what kind of angel are you? Or are you the devil?" said Sun and people applauded.

"You are the devil, damn Pirate!"

"Am I a pirate or a devil? Decide."

Sun saw Meltem was about to cry so he decided to back off.

"I was just joking, Angel, please forgive me!"

The words fell onto the F-key on the piano and Meltem felt his apology was as bad as his actions

"Don't make jokes about me!" She hit Sun's head with her small white bag.

Nicole came jumping over with a broom between her legs.

"What's happening here?" she asked as Dracula and Sleeping Beauty climbed down from the table.

The party host, Bora, was wearing a robot costume and had difficulty walking in it. Whispering into Meltem's ear, he said: "Guys, calm down. Meltem, I don't want any trouble at this party. Jack can give you a ride home if you want. Your home is on his way."

"Am I the guilty one? Okay, I'll leave then." On the verge of crying, she felt everyone was looking at her.

Nicole pulled her arm. "Where are you going?"

Bora waved to her and said, "Let her go!"

"She can't leave, she came here with me. I'll never let her go alone!"

Nicole and Meltem left the house, and Meltem began crying her eyes out. She was cold in her sleeveless dress so she wrapped her arms around herself. She wished she could fly with her wings.

"Shh! Angels don't cry. Let's wipe away your tears."

"Then the witches don't comfort people."

FOURTH SCENE

"My angel, let's stay for a while. I promise we'll leave in half an hour."

"You go inside. I'll wait here, Nik."

"Not here, it's cold. Come on, don't be a deal breaker," said Nicole, pushing her inside by her wings.

Meltem entered the gray Halloween-themed house, made a face and sat on a kitchen chair. There was skull shaped light on the table. A blond boy in a gardener costume approached her and offered the cup in his hand.

"Kahlua, Mexican coffee liquor. Do you want some?"

"No, thanks," replied Meltem sourly.

"Okay, your choice." He tossed it down, and then burped loudly before walking away, tittering.

Sun was still playing the piano in his pirate costume. Meltem felt hatred towards Bora. He was a family friend, but instead of supporting her he had wanted to make her leave. His behavior was like a robot's. Sometimes people became what they were wearing.

Meltem made eye contact with Nicole for a moment. Nicole smiled at her and climbed the stairs decorated with skulls, Tom following right after her. When she appeared again twenty minutes later her hat wasn't in its place, her buttons were undone and her hair was messy.

"You're finally here, young lady," Meltem expostulated. "Where are your hat and broomstick? Why has your hair gotten so messy?"

"I can't hear you."

Nicole pointed at her ears. Meltem spoke louder.

"Let's go!"

Noticing the plugs in Nicole's ears, Meltem continued: "First take them off, you witch. Now I've got you, traitor. That's why you don't mind all this noise, right? Why didn't you tell me? It's funny. Now we know why you haven't tied your hair up.

"Hush, it's a secret between us."

There was a panting sound: Sun had fainted. Everyone rushed to him while Bora dialed 911 and gave the address. Everything happened in a moment; the Halloween party ended up in the corridors of a hospital. Sun was in intensive care in an alcohol coma, and Bora was very angry as he had to deal with the police as the host of the party.

"I have called Sun's parents," he complained to Meltem, "but no one is answering the phone. What kind of parents are they? Yes, that is how it turns out if you give alcohol to a four-year-old kid. Moreover, his father says he can drink as much as he wants as long as he doesn't drive."

"Well, you're not very different, Bora." Meltem was still angry at him for his attitude toward her at the party. "It could have been you as well."

"No way, Meltem. I know when to stop."

"What does that mean?"

"There would be no one left alive if every person who drinks ended up in an alcohol coma."

"Strange that you assume every other person is like you."

"I don't. I just use my brain."

"I am surprised how you can when drunk."

"You were angry with me because of Sun and now you are protecting him. Two-faced Angel!"

"I think you should stop looking for someone else to blame."

Bora asked Nicole, "Am I to blame?" and waited for her to say no. Nicole was sleeping, her arms crossed and her mouth open; it had been a very tiring night and she usually didn't get enough sleep.

FOURTH SCENE

"When you get closer to something, it is hard to stop!" Meltem was staring at a spider on the wall. She got irritated as if she could feel it walking on her skin. She got that from her mother.

"It is also hard when you're not close."

"No, it's easy. If you're not close you stand still."

"You know so much, so I hope you also understand that being in an angel costume doesn't make you an angel."

"I have no intention of being an angel, Bora. I know it's only a costume, but you have become your costume. You left your brain somewhere."

"Oh my angel, you've lost your mind. Go drink your milk and sleep. You call us drunks? You've got drunk without drinking."

Meltem was silent. She had no more inclination to talk with Bora and would have slept all night at the hospital if Cihan hadn't woken her up.

Sun opened his eyes. A short nurse with a pink coat was changing his serum.

"Where am I?" he asked.

"You are at the hospital, young sir. Why did you drink that much at such a young age? Do you have a problem?"

"When I stop drinking I have to face the truth and I am afraid of it. That's why I put an alcohol mask on my face. Do you understand me?"

Sun turned his eyes away. That was also why he never held eye contact with anyone and couldn't speak without panicking. The nurse looked at the patient who put his sorrow into words like a poem. She could say nothing as she hadn't expected an answer like that.

"I'll let the doctor know that you are awake."

"Could you also let me know that I am awake?"

Alcatraz: Garbage

Just like a flicker, what she did was irritating her eye. There were unanswered questions in her mind. Letters were uneven, frail and so weak that they were not able to walk by themselves. Bizarre words, the result of these letters, formed a ball in her heart. This ball rolled around in her body and its oddness circulated as if it was blood.

Her soul smelled not of flowers but of garbage in almost all the rooms of her heart. The prison garbage truck came twice a week, honking inside her, but she did not hear it and did not open her door. All the garbage stayed inside.

One day after another, and then one week, then one year. Clean combined with dirty; her clean got dirty.

There was not a day without garbage. Inside her a sour, tatty smell was all around.

Maybe all she knew was the charm and shine of the things she had collected before they turned into garbage. Yet what she couldn't see was that the flashing light would never have been bright enough. Even though its entity was eternal, its reflection ultimately had an end. The flash was the half of its burning. It would be off as much as it would be on, no matter how long its life was.

She could not get clean. Even worse, she did not know how to get clean. Wet wipes dried while waiting unused, the package opened and the wetness gone. Sometimes a tissue was enough to clean the stain, but there were none anywhere, not even in the place she had kept them beforehand. The order of things was mixed. She couldn't find anything because of all the garbage. She should have put things in order according to their colors, shapes and purposes. She wanted to shake off whatever was on her hand, but it was stuck. She wiped it on her clothes, but then her clothes got dirty. Her hand messed up her clothes; her inside got all over her.

"When will the garbage truck pick up all this garbage?"

"Never," said the truck. "I no longer stop by for you. It has been months since there was last a dumpster in front of the door, so I guess no one lives here and pass by. I suppose you have removed your name from the list. I'm afraid you will have to throw it away bit by bit..."

"How on earth can I move this mountain of garbage?"

"It is you who has made the garbage up to this point and it is you who has not realized it as well…"

A yellow kitchen light was on in a cream one-story house on Oakland Grove Street. All the other parts of the house were dark as night. Julie was struggling among strange virtual creatures she was seeing for the first time in a black sea. The sky was torn apart with a horrendous noise. The tear was scarier than the noise itself.

As if she was in a place where all the garbage of the world collected, even a second was enough for her to want to rip off her nose. How come she was in such dirt? She could neither get out nor go into the waist-high water. Suddenly long dark-green moss began growing from her feet to the sky. She watched where it stretched, and then the moss quickly turned back and grabbed her throat. Like a big snake, somewhere in between an animal and a plant, it wrapped around her neck maybe ten times and then her neck got longer. Her arms and legs were stuck to the ground. Now she was a human creature resembling a giraffe.

"The most miserable times for a human are when they hide from themselves," she said to herself. "Whichever wardrobe you open, you find 'me'. Whenever you are in darkness, you can still see your mirror. Which nook is a cranny, can you tell?"

She gagged on the last drop in her throat. Her head between her arms, she was left in the dark. She hid herself under the wooden table, which she could only see thanks to a little light leaking between her arms. She rubbed her head against the wood as if she was sandpapering it, wanting to scratch the itchy part of her head on a rough place. First her runny nose, then her cheek, then her forehead...she picked the face of her truth bit by bit. What was her fault? Was there a fault in a place she knew? Which night was it on the calendar? Was it night again? But it was never day. All the days were going by without stopping at her place again. The time was jumping over her; the days were lost and she was brokenhearted. The sun beamed up the days into the night. As if her house was the only one with no light on, the whole neighborhood seemed to crack her with flashing lights.

It was the punishment for her silence. Knocking her head against the wall was not enough; it was impossible for her to cope with what she saw, so she chose the easy path: ignored it. She put her eyes out so as not to see anything and walked to her lies in that way. She became a sleepwalker; the nightmare was living next-door and it sometimes came to her for a coffee.

A woman's head with straggly hair and a flushed face dropped onto the kitchen table again. She was wearing a short-sleeved rhombus-shaped orange pullover. She sometimes raised her head, but it fell back onto her arms as if she couldn't carry it. She raised her right arm and smelled her armpit; she was sweating like a pig and gagged because of the smell.

Johnson had been six years old when he had asked Julie, "Why is this guy is still with us?" and he was about twelve when he had said, "This guy cannot be my dad, Mom!"

■

Treasure Island: The Aspects of Feelings

Lara was confused. There were young people in her street with advertising boards in their hands. They were changing their positions constantly to alter the direction of the arrows. These people were mostly wearing glasses, listening to music and dancing very well. They were on the move, jumping constantly, and the changing arrows were confusing people's minds. Lara was following the arrows as if she was following a table tennis match, but the advertisement people kept saying: "Go away from here, please!"

Lara wasn't able to interfere with the triangle of soul, mind and self. Everything had changed but her. Not being able to go on, she didn't. She wasn't even able to go back to the place she had come from.

SIXTH SCENE
(SUNDAY 6.45 P.M.)

Yasemin, guess where I went today. Yes, I went to the street on the card I've sent you—Lombard Street.

Curvy streets are inside us, just like veins. You follow the curves. Aren't our lives too curvy? Life curves, so do we; whenever it is straight, we become straight. We don't insist on going straight on a curvy road, which means we all follow the roads. Wherever the road leads us, we go there. The shape of our road shapes our lives. We cannot walk easily on a bad road. We cannot get our acts together unless our road is the right one. We go round curves one by one.

We can see the length of it, how short it is, but we cannot walk on it without going round the curves. Even though we think it is straight, while following it we realize it is not. We watch our feet on the road. Following a road is like shaping a balloon: you fear puncturing the balloon, but it is funny. And then, without realizing, you come to the end of the road.

On the road a lot of pictures are taken. Without knowing it you are present in many of them, even if you don't know the person who has taken them. In spy movies, the spy takes a photo of a smiling girl who is unaware. In the background there is suspense music. I can hear that music when I see the cameras on curvy roads.

SIXTH SCENE (SUNDAY 6.45 P.M.)

I have tons of photos, Yasemin. I wonder what photos are taken of me when I'm unaware. Where was I and what was I doing?

Isn't that interesting? Well, that's all…

(Saturday 11.04 a.m.)

Yasemin, hi!

San Francisco is a beautiful place. It looks like Istanbul a little bit. The Golden Gate—you know, we looked at its photos before I came here—kind of looks like The Bosporus Bridge. I think The Bosporus is much more beautiful. [Symbol]

(Monday 03.30 a.m.)

Yasemin, it's me again!

I've rented a flat with a Pakistani girl named Sadaf. She is a nice girl— but not as nice as you. The classes have been very intense these last few days, but I went to the movies last weekend with Cihan and Meltem. My mother's friend, Aunt Nuray, told me to bring my friend so Sadaf was also with us. It's good to have someone you know on the other side of the world. If it was not for Aunt Nuray, I would not be able to eat *mantı* and *sarmas*.

There are lots of homeless people, my dear Yasemin. Sometimes I feel very sorry for them. They have such tough lives because it is very cold at night. I get cold even with a jacket on, so think about them. With trolleys as their homes, they wander around the street. Don't say there are also lots of them in Istanbul, come here and see. The most interesting part is they don't play for sympathy. They carry written placards. I have seen one of them carrying a card with *Not gonna lie, I'll buy beer* written on it. I didn't know whether to laugh or cry.

Lots of love from the city with the red bridge.

Treasure Island: The Season of the Heart

The universe would be the color of a person's heart. When one sees the universe with their heart, it would be black, white or rainbow colored.

Cihan could see his actions reflected in the outer world. Sometimes they were good, and sometimes they were bad; sometimes they caused joy, other times sorrow. However he couldn't see his actions in his soul's mirror. When he complained about the storms inside him, it was he who was unaware of them. Was there really a storm?

The steel rope between his feelings and thoughts became a thin cotton one. His head and heart couldn't connect and swim in the swallow water. A strong wind made his heart a mess. He had to wear lots of things to warm it, but they were not enough. He had a hole inside and the cold was coming through it. He wouldn't be able to get warm as long as his heart was cold.

Cihan was worried. He cared and was interested in his heart, and as a result it became heavy. How could he perish under his own organ? How could the source of his life crush his head? He would have no escape other than to have a heart attack maybe. Would his heart riot against his body in this way?

Cihan was terrified of breaking hearts, but this caused him to break his own heart a hundred times. His body made excuses to do things its own way. His soul disobeyed its owner and lied about its own history.

There were some hearts that couldn't reach themselves and hear their own voices. When the emptiness echoed, they thought they had their answers. When they thought they were in the depths of pleasure, they were pushed back to their gardens.

SEVENTH SCENE

Every step he took while running, the land under his feet was slipping. He thought he was running just because someone was pulling the earth beneath him. He got addicted to running; every step automatically followed the last, pushing each other until Cihan couldn't stop.

He ran as if he would find his own self at the finish line. He got more and more ambitious when he felt the wind from the sea. He was in competition with himself and tried to reckon with himself. Running was good for him. He liked running as getting himself fit made him happy. He isolated himself from the outside world so much that he could see no one else while running a marathon. The other racers were just part of the décor, there to pump him up. In fact, he only ran for himself and to himself. It had been a long time since he had given running this meaning. He knew he could only find what he was looking for while running, yet he didn't know what was waiting for him at the end of the race. Sometimes he counted his steps, his breaths or sniffles. Running was his life.

In order to see the road, you must be on the road: words written in the latest book he had read. Cihan would be roadless if he looked at the road from a distance and he kept pushing himself to run because of that. He wanted the road to slide beneath his feet and had run in many different places. By doing that he prevented himself from falling.

SEVENTH SCENE

Cihan had been ignoring Edom's complaints. He didn't want to change the place they ran all the time; all he wanted to do was run on every road around the city, alone and without fuss. It was the same as wanting to walk on untouched snow.

Cihan began slowing down; he had finally got tired. Edom stopped right behind him on the seashore. Cihan leaned over and held his knees. His breathing got heavy; beads of sweat were on his face. He realized his shoelace was untied and bent over to tie it. When Edom arrived next to him, he didn't look up.

"You got tired very fast. We are supposed to run at least half an hour more."

He wiped his sweat on Cihan's shoulder.

"You go on."

"Okay, let's go slowly!" Edom tried to encourage him..

"I'm tired, not gonna continue. Don't insist, Edi!"

He walked to the grass area and got angry when he noticed that his shoelace was untied again. He took off his shoes and lay belly down on the grass. When the soil touched his lips, he had to spit twice. He turned sideways and put his hand under his head. Edom sat next to him, took out a bottle of water and drank it.

Hearing the water glug, Cihan wanted some.

"Give me some, my bottle is empty."

"I won't, it's mine."

"I'll take it anyway!"

Cihan took the bottle while it was still in Edom's mouth and the water spilt. Edom was wet and surprised.

"Hey, hey, hey, what's your problem?"

Cihan drank all the remaining water and threw the empty bottle at Edom, laughing at the same time. Why couldn't they share a light-blue water bottle? Edom rolled the bottle away and lay down on the grass, putting his hands under his head. Cihan lay down beside him and the two young men watched the sky in the park right next to the red bridge.

"Can you see the cloud under the abutments?" Cihan pointed it out. "The one right in the middle? It looks like an apple core. Interesting, right? I thought it looked like a ship at first."

"No, I think it is a dog. Look, he's opening his mouth wide to bark for a bone. And there is a big white cargo boat."

They both looked like they were writing in the air with their fingers. Edom pulled Cihan's finger down.

"Well, I can't see."

Cihan pushed Edom with his elbow.

"What are you doing?"

Edom clutched his hand to his heart as if it hurt.

"Edi, what's wrong? Don't exaggerate!"

Cihan got closer to Edom's face, anxiously waiting for him to open his eyes. Edom spat in his face and laughed loudly. Cihan stepped back as he got up.

Edom held out his hand. "That was a joke. Confess, it was a good one."

Cihan's expression changed. His retort stuck in his throat and he began running. He still didn't know whether he had reached himself.

EIGHTH SCENE

Şahin threw the paper on the rug. Meltem buried her face in her hands. She was sitting on the brown leather armchair in the living room, one of her legs tucked under her, anxiously waiting for her father to calm down.

Şahin kept saying the same thing over and over again.

"What are you feeling, shame? Why are you going to school? To study or to have fun? What's your problem? You have everything, do you need something else?"

He was like a thunderstorm above Meltem's head. Nuray touched Şahin's shoulder worriedly.

"Şahin, she is scared. Let's not give her a hard time."

"Don't get involved, woman!"

Meltem had not entered some of her exams and now there was a great uproar in the house. She couldn't speak; it was as if she had lost her tongue. Emir ran to his mother, crying, so Nuray took him and put him in his room.

Meltem whispered, "I'm sorry, Dad. I'm really sorry," but Şahin was still hot-headed. When the door opened, Meltem found herself praying for the first time in her life that it would be Cihan.

She was relieved when she heard his voice.

"I'm home! What's happening here?"

Şahin spoke only to Cihan; he saw his son as a younger version of himself.

"Cihan, take of your sister. Her grades are terrible, so she should study night and day. Look here, all of you watch your steps! Don't make me get mad!"

"Okay, Dad. All right, come away." Cihan pushed his father gently out of the room. Şahin smoothed the few hairs on his head and put his round glasses in his shirt pocket. Despite his big belly, he wore tight pants so he had to keep loosening his belt. While he was adjusting his belt, his shirt gaped open a little and his hairy bellybutton was visible.

"When I come back from Paris, we'll have a talk again, young lady. Wait for it!"

"Okay, Dad. I'll take care of her."

Emir had put all his toys into a small truck. He took them to the stairs and threw them down one by one.

"Bombs. Let the war begin! *Dishhh*! *Aiaiai*!"

Nuray took Emir's hand.

"Dear look, you've broken them. We cannot buy new ones."

Emir ignored his mother and ran up and down a couple of times. Nuray sometimes got tired simply by following him with her eyes. He ran so fast and was on the move all the time.

Şahin was angry, Nuray thought, but he wasn't the kind of guy to get that mad at Meltem. Something must have happened at the office; even though he never told Nuray anything, she could tell. There would be some incident on the way—Nuray concluded that from her leg pain. It would happen soon, and it would happen whether she wanted it to or not.

NINTH SCENE

Dozens of tiny people were doing acrobatics. All these tiny people spoke various languages; every one of them had different ideas. Despite that, they formed a world that was a human; they all formed a human body, and that human turned around his own axis. His head was a dormitory for the tiny people that formed him. When the sun rose, the tiny people went to their jobs around the body. When it was time to go to bed, they came back to their beds in the head.

There was a knock on the door. Johnson found a man with a fedora and a briefcase holding up a child in pajamas.

"Was it you who did not let the child in?" he asked, his chin pointing upwards.

"Yes, because he causes headaches. There is so much noise when he comes inside and everyone complains about it."

The detective put his cigar out on the wall. The wall absorbed the heat. He and the child entered.

"Sleep Child, hold my hand!"

Johnson didn't resist. Sleep Child was playing with a truck in his bed, which was in Johnson's head. He didn't mind a pillow fight; things he did were like keeping a diary for him—*I searched the dumpsters, went to the beach, went along to the bridge, ate bread in a restaurant kitchen, went to the shelter, collected a tin, peed on the wall, wrote on the sidewalk, etc.* The only thing he couldn't resist was the truck. When Sleep Child whined it was okay, but when he began playing with the truck, Johnson tore his hair out. He wanted to pluck his thin braids. He was willing to do anything as long as Sleep Child would leave him.

One day, Sleep Child uprooted a tree and brought it to him in the middle of the night. The roots of the tree wrapped around him. The tree looked as if it had been uprooted only a little while ago as mud was dropping onto the ground. Sleep Child had turned that night into a nightmare for him. Sleeping was only possible without feeling any pain. He had never slept with a merciless monster.

Johnson was lying on a green mattress in Streetlight Shelter. There were fifty-three people including him there—that was what was written on the door of the room they were sleeping in. Johnson was a countable being. If it was not for him, there would be fifty-two people in that room. His existence was an entity, he was real. He liked that as no one counted him on the street. It was worth sleeping there to be realized; it was good to be counted, and in one way it meant he was esteemed.

He was sleeping on a mattress that was intended for rich people to do sports on. His whole body had surrendered to sleep. He slept into the night, unlike his sleep for the last three nights. He'd had to sleep in an abandoned car, but the nights had been extremely cold. If he had not slept in that windowless car, he would have frozen and died. If the police had learned that the car had been abandoned, he would have been in trouble.

He smelled something bad: somebody must have had the runs. He stopped breathing from his nose; he had to open his mouth. The shit on him seemed almost as though it was not on him.

A chorus of coughing began, just as it did every night. The wheezy coughs were followed by dry coughs. Some of them lasted a long time while the others were short. One coughing fit was so

NINTH SCENE

severe that Johnson thought the victim of it was dying. Some of the homeless had no sheets as they were in the washing machine. All you got when you slept under this roof was a pillow and a blanket, and to be counted.

Johnson went to the person next to him and shook his right shoulder. It was a young man, sleeping in his jacket.

"Hey, wake up, buddy. Drink some water!"

The young man opened his eyes. "Go away!"

When Johnson lay back down on the bed, he put his hands between his legs. He always tied himself down at night so that he could not escape from himself. Johnson was afraid of his dreams. That was why everything was his skin's color—when he was asleep hope left the building.

It was good being able to lie down. Although he was homeless, he was lucky to be able to lie down that night.

Everything would be fine if Sleep Child did not come and sleep arrived instead.

TENTH SCENE

Şahin was pissed off by the look that the man across from him gave Linda. The young mustached guy was wearing torn jeans and a saucy smile. He was chewing gum, and all these things got on Şahin's nerves. He began stamping his feet and gritting his teeth. Whenever he got angry he vibrated his left foot, and his belly and the seat also began vibrating.

Linda stood out everywhere she went with her long blond hair, hourglass figure and color changing eyes with long eyelashes. She had gotten used to drawing attention. She didn't mind being the center of attention much; she even liked it.

She was coquettishly showing some photos to Şahin, the man she loved.

"That's a nice photo. No, I don't like that. That's a so-so one. I look like I am buck-toothed here, why did you have to be that close when you took it?"

Şahin ignored her remarks. Finally he couldn't stand it anymore and stood up. Taking a step towards the target, he held onto the pole, stretched out his bald head and raised his hand in a threatening way.

"Stop looking at her, Bro!"

TENTH SCENE

For Şahin, the young man was not in the metro but in court. The young man blew up like a balloon then looked up, angry at Şahin's attitude towards him.

He answered in broken English, "Not your business, old man. Go your way. You found a beautiful girl. Oh, you can have her, but we cannot?"

"You're at my mercy!"

Şahin descended upon him. Suddenly they were surrounded by people. A white-haired, tall and thin old woman with a black jacket said gently, "*Au secours, s'il vous plaît de l'aide!*" (Help please!)

The man in a suit next to her yelled, "*Il y a un combat ici.*" (There is a fight here!)

Linda stood up in a rush and pulled Şahin back.

"Şahin, please stop it!"

"*S'il vous plait, arrêté! Que quelqu'un les arrête!*» (Somebody please stop them!)

"*C'est de la folie!*" (This is madness!)

Linda could speak French very well so the company always sent her to meetings in Europe

The young man was shocked by a punch on the head.

"Act your age!" he said and kicked Şahin in the leg. Then he twisted Şahin's arm and ran away, leaving Şahin lying on the ground. When they came into the station he was rushed to first aid.

Şahin called home two days afterwards to inform Nuray that he had hurt his arm and would stay in Paris a couple more days. When Şahin sensed Nuray's concern, he tried to calm her down but actually added salt to the wound.

"Don't worry about me, Nuray. The meeting finished yesterday and the other group members flew to Las Vegas. I guess we will come back on Sunday. I'm not alone, anyway, my colleague is here with me. Don't worry, she will take care of me."

"Which colleague?"

"Linda. You ask as if you know all of them. Now, I should hang up, the nurse is coming. *Hadi!*"

Şahin had never say goodbye, he always said *hadi* in Turkish when he hung up the phone. A cold and dull *hadi* was always his last word. Whenever Nuray tried to say something after it, he would begin extending the *hadi*.

"*Hadiiii...hadiiiiiiii...*" then he would suddenly hang up.

Nuray got a migraine. Her head began getting warmer with a prickling sensation. She remembered her leg pain—here comes the rain. More than that, she sensed a flood coming. She felt that, yet she had so much to learn.

Alcatraz: Heart—The Boss

Lara's heart was hurt by love as well as Lara herself. She listened her heart and heard the echoes of the sentence: "*I am the boss!*"

Hundreds of dwarfs were carrying blood in their tiny buckets. In this big factory, there was recirculation all the time; the inside was cleaned with red water constantly. Machines in various sizes and gear wells were all around. At certain times the tubes were filled with food and dwarfs' duty was to divide and arrange it. There was a separate section for the waste. The stomach's rumble was heard much more intensely inside and the dwarfs sometimes dropped their buckets.

All these processes were different in different beings. There were no interventions during the processes: they were all the product of a structured body. Even when a human slept, there was a light on in the boss's room. The heart boss kept working all night, studying and reading. Research was going on all the time, printing of web pages and trying to understand the ego. The boss was looking for ways to reach the human. His duty was to provide the soul with essentials. From the moment he had been put in charge of the factory, all he had done was work, study and research. The heart's only struggle was to put the factory's learning to good use. Despite working for the body, in fact the heart was working for the soul, collaborating with the mind to produce new methods.

The heart only smiled when the new methods were comprehended and internalized, otherwise the heart was worried. When there was a revolution on the left side of the breast, the body went on strike. When love came to someone, the heart either struck at the cause, making life miserable, or let the owner of the cause fall in love.

Lara opened the letter from her heart.

You forgot about me. It has been days since you looked at your heart. I won't expostulate, but I feel a little hurt. When you say to someone, "You broke my heart" it's actually you who is breaking me. It's you who hurts me most in this confined body. I beat in your name, but you take other steps. Maybe today, maybe tomorrow or a month or a year after you'll hear me. You are afraid of death and say, "Don't leave me, keep beating" which means you are aware of death. Yet you still ignore it. You plan your future even if you are not sure the future will come. Who do you hold onto when you are without a lifesaver in a sea of materials? Neither the sea nor the actions are yours.

It's only me taking steps. You need to take one too.

I'll catch you. I promise to do that.

Don't leave me alone in this borrowed body.

Your breathing gets less and less, so do you.

Please take a step to become more.

ELEVENTH SCENE

Lara described herself as an *Istanbul lady* in her school yearbook. She carried Istanbul in her heart like a lover. Nobody knew she had brought a city with her to San Francisco. Lara loved her lover's Istanbul side, and her lover was as far away from her as Istanbul itself. She had gotten used to it, but at first she hadn't wanted to leave the city her lover loved. Istanbul opened her eyes. Being far away physically was the same as being far away mentally.

Maybe that was what she couldn't escape. She couldn't leave what was inside her: she was still in love with Taner even though he was married to another woman. She had to give up this love; everyone around her advised her to do so.

"*Still* Lara? Forget that guy already!"

She decided to erase the word *still* from her vocabulary.

Lara had met Eylül when she went to Taner's house for dinner. Eylül was a small but very pretty woman. Being lovely, kind-hearted and merry, she was the kind of woman that no man could resist. Lara remembered the shock and disappointment when she had first learned that Taner was married. She hadn't been able to eat anything and escaped to the bathroom by pretending to be sick.

Yasemin had admonished her in the elevator.

"What happened to you, Lara, are you crazy? We disgraced ourselves. Before coming here you seemed okay, so why did you keep going to the bathroom? When you saw Eylül, you froze. Have you met her before?"

"No, I just learned that the guy I love is married."

Lara rushed to the faculty of arts and sciences next day. She had to catch Taner before he entered the class and had opened the door without knocking for the first time ever.

Taner was on the phone. When he saw Lara, he cut the conversation short.

"A student is here. I'll call you later, Mr. Hasan."

Lara was looking at the books, the chair she was on and the unsteady table she and Taner studied at together. She recalled how Taner had made her laugh when he hit his head on the table while trying to adjust its leg. Remembering, she calmed down a little bit. New scenes were unfolding before her eyes, though. When they were eating fish in Eminönü, a small fish bone had stuck inside her mouth and Taner had pretended to be a doctor, making her open her mouth. She had gone breathless as if she had been running a lot.

Taner hung up the phone and looked at Lara with questioning eyes. Then he tapped the table with his hand as if he had just remembered something.

"Are you better now? I'm so sorry about last night. Maybe it would be better if you saw a doctor today."

"You didn't tell me!" Lara sat down without asking first. There was pain in her voice. Despite her looking calm, there was a storm inside her.

"Didn't tell you what?"

"Stop pretending. That you're married, of course!" Opening her big eyes wider, she could not hide her anger anymore.

ELEVENTH SCENE

Taner lowered his voice so as not to be heard from outside. Moving his hands as if conducting an orchestra, he tried to control her reaction.

"Lara, calm down, dear. Didn't you know that?"

"Of course not. How could I? You never told me!" She pulled her chair closer to the table. "You haven't even acted as if you're married. Plus, please don't call me dear again."

"Oh you are concerned about that, dear? I call everyone dear. I've got used to it. You haven't missed much, we have only been married for a year."

He leaned back lazily, adjusted the collars of his shirt and pushed his chair away from the table. The situation was serious; he hadn't been expecting this reaction. He looked at her almost jealously.

Lara was wearing beige jeans and a black T-shirt. Her armpits were wet because of the heat of the moment. She was silent, but what she had gone through was all stirred up inside. Her thesis advisor had toyed with her feelings, but she was sure that he also felt something for her. Otherwise she wouldn't be in such bad state now. He had encouraged her love to grow.

"You intentionally invited me to dinner to find out, didn't you. I guess your wife doesn't know that we went to the movies and dinner."

"Lara, you are misunderstanding. I only want you to work on your thesis better..."

There was a knock at the door. A short brown-haired guy with a goatee asked, "Professor, are you going to the class?"

"In a minute."

He picked up his notes and heavy books.

"Lara, we'll talk later."

Lara had just stood there, staring blankly at her love. The corridors of the university turned into the corridors of a prison. Taner became like a lawyer, coming to see her on visiting day, saying: "I can't do anything for you. Only the judge can decide if life improves."

*

Lara was in an unrecognized love, but she believed in the existence of this love. It was something unnamed; it couldn't be seen or touched. She couldn't show it; there was only one moment of proof.

That moment happened in Çamlıca Hill. Istanbul had witnessed Taner look at Lara. He had looked into her eyes and something had awoken in her heart. Moreover, he had decided to look at her instead of the huge city. Lara's face had blushed to the ears; she hadn't known where to put her hands

Lara's fingers burned on the hot tea glass she was holding.

"I'm going to the U.S.A. I got accepted to the master's program in San Francisco, but I couldn't leave without seeing you."

She locked her eyes onto him as if to say "Deal with it."

"Is there someone you know there?"

Taner called for another tea with a hand sign.

"My mom has a friend there called Nuray. We'll meet up when I get there. Why do you ask?"

"No reason, only that it's the other side of the world."

Lara murmured, "When a person is lonely inside, it doesn't matter if she is on the other side of the world."

"Excuse me?"

"Never mind!"

The short waiter with stubbly beard left two glasses of tea on the table.

ELEVENTH SCENE

"I'm not gonna drink it. Please take it." Lara pushed the glass.

"Your wife doesn't like tea. It's a pity!"

"She isn't my wife. I have a wife, but this is not she. Be careful!"

Lara couldn't help but laugh. While laughing hysterically, she was wiping her eyes and nose.

Taner locked his eyes on a guy in the corner smoking a hookah. The smoke traveled to their table on the wind and they smelled the apple aroma. Taner was looking at anything except Lara.

"I cannot tell you not to leave as you know about Eylül..."

He bit his lips, leaving only his thin mustache visible. Lara's brown eyes were full of tears. Then he opened the sugar bowl and put three more sugars into tea which was almost finished. His words were so bitter that he tried to make them sweeter with sugar.

From that day on, Lara learned that sugar was only a fake sweetener. She stopped taking sugar in her tea.

*

Feeling sorry for herself in love seemed almost like hatred, but actually she wanted to change. She wanted to regenerate in another body with another heart. She wanted to be born again. Or she wanted to do all that, but couldn't confess to it. Someone said love was like being born again; she replied that love was a rebirth of herself from herself. She was loveless. She had brought a whole city with her, but her lover was with another. She had engraved the image of the evening in Taner's apartment in her memory and she carried it with her everywhere. She wanted this image to be broken and not broken at the same time. She remembered how she used to bounce on the top of the clouds whenever she heard the voice of her love and realized there was actually no voice on the top of the clouds. To see him for just a few hours she had made up many stories.

"I want to get his attention, only his attention. I want him to look at me, hear me, think about me and always talk about me. I want his last words before sleeping to be my name, and in the morning his first words to be my name too. He would love me so much that I would define myself in him as crazy and calm. I would be lost, then found and lost again. I would know my deep and my shallow. He would recognize me in a million people, distinguish me easily. Only he would hold my hand. He would be only mine. I would give him every song and my scent would stay on him. I would see him falling and rising from my love. When he is exhausted, I would crown his exhaustion with my love. He would burn with the fire of love and I would bring him water, but not to extinguish the fire. I would not want his fire to die.

Lara hadn't told anybody why she left her master's unfinished and went to the U.S.A. She also told no one why she didn't work with Taner anymore. She was not able to carry on living in the same city as the married guy whom she loved. Taner was married to Eylül already, and Lara was married to a season of sorrow.

*

When Taner entered his room he saw a white envelope next to his black leather notebook. There was no name on it. He immediately tore it and skimmed through it.

When love first came, it wasn't playing drums in the street of heart. First, it seemed as a wounded gazelle or a small child who has lost everything in an earthquake. It stood in the corner in such a naive way. If nobody touched it, maybe sorrow would have left it there. Love begins when you notice it. When there is something and that something is right, the naive child whines. The more you feed that child, the more he become a part of you. When love wants to leave, you give everything not to let it go. It is you who is naive, not love. It is love who stays, but you have already left the place.

TWELFTH SCENE

Nuray squeezed the phone between her left ear and shoulder. She turned on the tap and ran three drops of aloe vera under it. The last one splashed on her and she wiped the green spot.

"What? Should I take Emir to doctor? What's wrong with my son?"

"His kindergarten teacher called again because of his problems: attention deficit, hyperactivity, constant talking, not being able to stand still."

"You scared me, Şahin. These are usual things."

"His usual misbehaving, yes, but we have been told that we should see a doctor."

"Okay, I will call the doctor tomorrow then."

"Don't call tomorrow, call now!"

"Okay, I'll call now."

"*Hadiii.*"

Nuray had made Meltem wear the traditional dress which she had worn on her Henna night. She had finally persuaded Meltem to wear it by saying an introduction in costume would be very effective. Watching Meltem leaving her room complaining, Nuray's eyes filled with tears. It felt like only yesterday that she was crawling, yet she was now of an age to get married.

Gold thread gave a different look to Meltem's thin, long and dark figure. Meltem didn't get why her mother had brought her Henna night dress, which was two sizes too small for her, from Konya to all the way to America. She didn't know how to wear the pink kerchief. Her mother was the one who adjusted it.

"Okay, Mom, I will take it off in half an hour anyway. Plus who will know whether it's the right way?" She gathered her skirts and went down the stairs. "What feels ordinary to you is different for foreigners."

Nuray got angry with Meltem's indifference. This was a huge honor, but her daughter was not aware of that. Nuray walked towards the countertop, opened the fridge and took out the baklava. She ate one of them immediately.

"Delicious!"

Nuray was watching her daughter eating her cereal, waiting for approval.

"Mom, how can I possibly carry this? It'll spoil my dress."

"Nothing will happen. I'll come with you."

She placed all baklava pieces on the plate and walked to the door. She wanted to get in the car without drawing any attention and spilling the sherbet from the baklava.

"Mom, I'll go by myself."

You were only a babe in the woods yesterday, when did you grow up? Nuray said silently and put on her navy blue satin hair band.

"I'm ready," Nuray said in a voice that brooked no argument.

"Mom, what do you have in that bag?" asked Meltem, looking at the mirror.

"You look very beautiful, darling" said Nuray. She wanted to change the subject, but then decided not to. "This? Nothing, just some bed clothes and tablecloths that I embroidered. We'll put them on display, too."

Nuray would be happy for a successful introduction to tell her relatives in Turkey about. Meltem rushed to the car, ignoring her mother who ran after her to hold her dress.

When Meltem opened the door of the smoky jeep, she said, "Mom, it will be a very tiny stand. How will we put all this stuff there? It will be a short introduction anyway. A couple of hours maybe. Don't make a big fuss."

Nuray was hurt. The patterns she had embroidered were her only consolation. Nuray wanted them to be seen by other people, yet even her own daughter made fun of her. She put the bag back in the house with a lump in her throat. Watching her mom, Meltem felt sorry for her.

"Mom, don't hide them. Put them on the tables, people will see them and you'll be happy!"

She tried to atone, but it only made Nuray feel worse. Meltem got into the car, but Nuray didn't want to go anymore.

"Mom, I'm going. You?"

"Go. I'll go for a walk."

Nuray was sad about Meltem's ignorance of her own culture. She had been born and raised in America and only went to Turkey in the summer for a month. Maybe the problem was that Nuray hadn't taught her culture enough. Meltem didn't speak Turkish well; Şahin saw no point in teaching it, so Meltem only talked in Turkish with Nuray. Only Cihan liked talking in Turkish, maybe because he had been born there.

Nuray's first pregnancy had been problematic so she'd had to lie down all the time. She stayed with her mother in Konya and Cihan had been born there. Şahin had been very upset about not being there during the delivery and he named his son over the phone.

Nuray was only able to return to San Francisco after three months, which might have been why there was distance between Cihan and his father. Nuray was quick to make connections between incidents, and she often talked to herself. In the past people may have called her crazy, but now everyone talked on the phone without putting it to their ears.

*

Meltem didn't really want to attend the cultural festival at the college, but when her history professor told her he would give extra credit to those who attended she decided to do so. Extra credit meant everything as when she got it her father would do anything she wanted. As the only Turkish student, Meltem prepared her own stand for the festival. She hung up a Turkish flag and the tablecloths, towels and veils, and laid out some coffee cups and a painting of Turkish paper marbling.

The schoolyard was crowded. There was traditional music of every culture coming from every stand. The stand next to her was *Brasilia* and they were playing fast Brazilian music and dancing. There was Syria on the other side of her with two dark guys in whites explaining something on the map. She looked at her own map and repeated the information she had read about Turkey as people came up to her stand and asked her about the baklava and her dress. Meltem thought the information sheets she had prepared and the history would draw more attention, but instead the people were in line to take a photo of her in her traditional dress.

Everybody seemed very interested in Turkey. She kept hearing the same sentence:

"I'd really like to visit there."

Meltem was surprised at this interest. She questioned herself, as for the last few years she had stayed in the U.S.A. instead of visiting Turkey. She hadn't realized how lucky she was. She was Turkish and she became aware of it while telling others about her culture. She imagined a tree with branches all over the world. The distance was no excuse as the branches could carry the fruit everywhere.

THIRTEENTH SCENE

Reb and Mariana got out of the taxi and entered San Francisco International Airport hand in hand.

"Mom, why we are here?"

"Maybe we'll go to Mexico to visit your grandpa," said Reb on the elevator

"We both know it's not true, Mom."

At the same time an old lady with gray hair complimented Mariana.

"I really like your jacket!" Maybe that was her way of changing the subject so she didn't have to intervene in other people's private lives.

"Thank you!"

When the elevator doors opened, mother and daughter pulled out their baggage. Reb was walking fast.

"Mom, slow down please. I don't have long legs like you."

Reb stopped. She didn't even know where her destination was. She felt if she ran fast enough, her pain would go faster. She would wake up from her nightmare. Without saying anything, she grabbed Mariana's hand and went on her way.

"Mom, I'm tired."

"Mom, I have to pee."

THIRTEENTH SCENE

"Mom, I'm hungry."

Reb finally stopped.

"Are you hungry? Then I will buy you a pizza."

"Okay," said Mariana, feeling slightly ashamed.

Reb and Mariana were sitting at a small round table in a café, watching the planes. Reb bought only one slice of pizza, and Mariana didn't ask why as she knew her mother didn't have any money.

So as not to upset her mother, she said, "You can take a bite, Mom."

Reb smiled at her.

"Mom, why are we here?"

"It's rainy outside, Mariana. We will stay here for a few days. I have an idea—why don't we play the airport home game?"

Her happiness was so fake that she was embarrassed.

Mariana was playing with her mom's wrist pin, small and white just like her hands.

"Mom, we are homeless, aren't we. The guy on the bus told me he was traveling all the time by bus because of the cold. I know we don't have a place to stay. Please tell me the truth."

Reb held her daughter's tiny hands and kissed them. Her tears touched Mariana's hands. She hugged her firmly again and again. When she hugged her daughter, the pain diminished a little bit. She felt empowered by her daughter

"We don't have a home, Mariana, but we'll have one soon. Don't get upset!"

"Don't cry, Mom, I only feel sorry for you. Otherwise I'm happy. Look, I'm smiling."

She opened her red lips and her white teeth were visible.

Reb and Mariana stayed entwined for a long time and recharged each other. They united the power of their love and gathered breath from each other. This was not an uncommon thing to see in an airport, but it was the beginning of hard times for them.

Reb had thought about every possibility before leaving home and had called five shelters. They had all rejected them. The airports were the best place to stay, according to a few web pages. She had read the comment: *There are long waiting lists for the shelters and you only have one week there even if they do give you a bed. There is also a possibility of getting fleas*, and then she had decided to go to the airport first. They could not take a shower, but they would have a place to stay. I didn't matter to Reb whether she had a roof over her head, but it was important for Mariana. February was cold.

Now they did have a roof over their heads, but it was not home. For those who had nowhere to go, it was painful to be in the home of the planes watching people who did have somewhere to go. It was just like a starving person's desperation when they looked at other people eating. Reb felt the pain of a bird stuck in a cage.

For a homeless person, staying at an airport was like being breathless. Humans couldn't live without breath. If her daughter hadn't called her Mom, she would already have been giving up on life. As a mom, though, she had to live twice.

Mariana and Reb changed lounges, and after midnight they lay down in the quietest one.

"Mom?"

"Yes, Mariana."

"Have you slept yet?"

"No, but why are you not sleeping?"

"The seat is so hard, I feel like I'm falling. "

"Don't be afraid, I'm here. Close your eyes."

Reb draped her legs over the seat and covered herself with her jacket. Her vacant look froze on the vacant seats. She'd had one more shelter to try calling, but then her battery had died.

Mariana hadn't forgotten.

"Are you going to call that number, Mom?"

"Okay, I'll call."

"Promise me!"

"Promise, sleep well!"

"Mom?"

"What now?"

"Does the plane enter here?"

"No!"

Alcatraz: Loneliness

Lara was proceeding in her mind, hand in hand with anxiety, fear and curiosity. Her mind and heart had become friends. The most interesting feeling was when she opened a closed door and met a new thing. It was time to open the door of loneliness. When she opened the door, she saw the room was empty. The doors inside began talking to her.

"When you take a city off once, you cannot wear it anymore. When you are in another place you feel foreign, but become friends with yourself. Finally, when you have no power to look outside, you bend inside. Bending hurts your hands, arms, legs, and most of all your heart. Like a bow, you stretch a lot, and then come back to your crumpled self. You get used to this state and spend your days wearing it. This color doesn't match with some parts of you, but you embrace it.

"Getting used to something is not worse than being lonely. Has it happened to you too? Have you felt lost when your country and your loved ones have stopped holding your hand? Have you called them, crying? Have you realized that you are an adult now?

"Why do you want to grow up, get lonely and strange? Calling out for loneliness is like calling to a catastrophe with passion. You want them to come and sit with you, but not make small talk, just gaze at the TV. You only need to know they are here and there is no danger ahead. Actually there are lots of dangers, but you can't see from there. After you have become a stranger to yourself, you can look but not see. It is spicier than ignoring, but you cannot taste the meal as the spices have lost their taste. When you are tasteless, strangers welcome you. There is no one local here. Wherever you look, there are strangers."

FOURTEENTH SCENE

Lara wanted to know what it would be like to stay in the places that she had to pass. She wondered how her soul would react when the safety that had always been there was not there anymore. The doors were not closed to the street, but the streets closed their doors to the homeless. The streets were not enough for her; she needed to be in minds of the people on the street to feel the loneliness they felt. This was important for her as she wanted to reflect their truth in her paper.

Professor Richard had told them, "You will get better grades if you can prepare a real and believable project."

When it got darker, Lara's heart beat faster. With every heartbeat her body trembled. She said goodbye to her warm bed and her home. Her desire was to write about desperation by being desperate and to welcome the morning where she would be the loneliest, but she didn't know how to pretend to be someone she wasn't. She wasn't desperate; she had the keys of both her car and her house in her pocket. Although there was a home she could escape to, she would have to pretend not to have the keys.

Her big hazel eyes looked around for homeless people. She was determined not to run away. She wanted to wait until the sunlight to be able to understand. Lara was walking quietly with a backpack, wearing a thick jacket, a black hat and combat boots. She comprehended why people with a lot of sorrow were so quite; the noise of

FOURTEENTH SCENE

the silence scared her. She couldn't hear the outer noise because of the noise of her heart. There were endless sirens inside her.

Lara was walking to Buena Vista Park with slow steps. It was already cold; she could feel it even before she tried to sleep, and she didn't know how cold the night would turn. She placed her backpack on one of the benches near the tennis court and gazed at the trees without knowing what she was waiting for. She realized for the first time how big and scary the trees were; the song of the birds sounded like the opening credits of a horror movie. If her mother had known what she was doing, she would have immediately come over and dragged her back to Istanbul. What she was doing was an ultimate craziness, but Lara loved the excitement the project was presenting.

There was someone lying on the bench a few meters away. That was what she was looking for. She had nothing that was likely to be stolen, and she had a pocket knife that she could use in an emergency, but even thinking about that possibility scared her.

The stranger lying on the bench stood up slowly. Lara was looking at her, but trying not to seem as though she was looking. She caressed her shoulders and glanced at the dark old woman, then took a deep breath. The homeless woman began shuffling towards Lara. Lara checked her pocket knife and held it. With her other hand she smoothed her clothes. Sometimes adjusting her clothes was a way to distract herself or hide her shyness or fear.

The woman seemed like a native homeless. She had a trolley full of things and folded her hands behind her back as if on a patrol. The woman was walking and every step fed Lara's regret; the four or five meters seemed more like kilometers. She thought about running away and tried to figure out how long it would take her to leave the park, but then thought, *She is your grandma's age. Calm down, you can handle it.*

The woman stopped in front of Lara and said, "Give me cigarette."

"I don't have one. I don't smoke."

"Okay, then give me money."

Lara couldn't say anything. She had left her purse at home and taken only ten dollars with her. Her car was parked thirty minutes away and she had walked from Bueno Vista.

The woman lowered her hand but still stood there.

"Why you are here?"

"Excuse me?"

"Go, leave now! You are a new face, very inexperienced. You'll be wasted here. They're gonna come soon."

"Who is gonna come?" Without waiting for an answer, she added, "No, I don't want to go anywhere."

Lara said this last sentence to make herself believe that she would not leave. Although it was cold, she was sweating.

"There is no place for you to sleep here. All these benches have owners. Go away!"

Lara said, "But this bench is empty."

"For now."

Lara sat back on the bench and exhaled. She would write everything as it happened that night. She was looking for a torch inside her backpack, but she couldn't find anything as she had stuffed thick clothes inside. The woman was right: this place belonged to the homeless, not to her. The homesickness she felt was not loneliness. She had a roommate; a mother to whom she talked every day; friends and relatives in Istanbul. There was always huge love waiting for her in Istanbul.

FOURTEENTH SCENE

She was not lonely and she was safe, but at that time with a homeless stranger, she found her loneliness. She found what she was going to write.

With her torch in her left hand, she began writing in the notebook on her lap. She usually wrote in small italics, but now she was writing without paying any attention. The letters lost their way, just like a homeless person.

Homeless told me to leave. She said, "You have no place here. That place is not yours. You do not belong here and this place doesn't belong to you." I cannot leave now as there is a galloping horse inside me. It would be the death of me. I have to wait for that horse to calm down, slow down, then I can dismount. I took a risk, I taped the mouth of the fear. Whatever the fear says, I don't hear it. I am lying on a bench with my legs near my stomach. It is cold, dark and scary, but I still want to meet the ones who call this place home. Do I have a death wish? If death wishes to have me, will it leave without taking me? My grandma always says "Whatever will be, will be". Let's see what will happen. Who will die in the end? Will I be able to see tomorrow? I'm deep in the night; I'm dark as the night. I have tied my hands. I hear a deep laughing and I wait for my moment to see. Come on, my reality, make yourself visible to me!

Then, Lara heard swearing behind her and smelled rotten potato. She immediately put her notebook in her backpack.

"Hey, man, we have a guest here!" yelled a big man, holding his thick quilt on his back like a turtle. There was another man next to him, short and middle-aged.

"Well, when I came here, it was empty. So..."

"Meow, meow, kitty cat."

Lara took up her backpack to go to another bench, but before she could take a step the huge guy pushed her back down.

"Kitty, you're our guest tonight." He laughed loudly. If there had been mountains around, the whole city would have echoed. Or maybe Lara became as large as the city and took the sound inside her so it could unite with her fear in a moment.

Lara checked her pocket knife and took it out with one move. She hurled it at the man's arm. Even she couldn't believe her readiness. Now the night was bleeding, she knew her moment.

The man was taken by surprise and Lara took the opportunity to run. She left everything behind—her backpack, notebook, everything. The cut wasn't that deep, but the blood spouted out of it.

She was running, out of breath. Running every morning had worked out very well. If she had a place in the marathon like Cihan, she would record a good time. She felt proud of herself. Finally she stopped. There was a flow of sweat down her back. She bent forward and saw a pair of white sneakers. Her eyes traveled up and she saw ripped jeans, a half closed zipper and finally a stranger touched her face. An African-American man with long braided hair and blue eyes was standing beside her. His face was illuminated in the dark night, but it was not clean.

Lara decided she had jumped out of the frying pan into the fire.

Alcatraz: The Rain Curtain

Cihan was trapped in a waterfall; he couldn't see a thing. He opened his eyes wide. His whole face became an eye, yet still he couldn't see because there was a rain curtain before him. He opened his eyes again, yet he was still trapped in water. He was going under without seeing. He became blind and small, leaving him clueless. He encountered surprise rains all the time; the rain was a grace, yet sometimes it got together with the wind and carried dirt. The wind was beating and the rain was crying instead of him. Who had tied his hands? Who had made him get into this car? The despair burned his nose. It was a nightmare not being able to escape from his eyes. While he was running away from the rain, his own self had caught him.

FIFTEENTH SCENE

It wasn't snowing in San Francisco. The best place to ski was Lake Tahoe, where the mountains and the lake met between Nevada and California. Edom sent one of the ski resort brochures to Cihan to persuade him to go there.

"Wondering what heaven is like? Lake Tahoe awaits you!"

Cihan was waiting for Edom to arrive at six. When a black jeep turned around the corner, he yelled to his mother, "Mom, Edom is here. I'm going!"

The car stopped in front of the green house on Turk Street.

"Edom's car is lemon, isn't it?"

"Yes, Mom, that's Rannan Mandel's jeep."

"How did Edi persuaded his tight dad to lend it him?"

"Please, Mom."

"Okay, I said nothing." Nuray zipped her lips.

Cihan put on his brown scarf and hat. He kissed his mom, who was waiting with a lunch box. Nuray didn't sleep much, so she had made sarmas and also lentil balls. Cihan laughed at her fussing over the buns.

"I baked some pastry yesterday so that I could do the other stuff. They won't get stale, *inshallah*."

FIFTEENTH SCENE

"Mom, calm down. You didn't have to stay up all night to make these sarmas just because Edi loves them."

"I made them for both of you, son."

Nuray caressed his son's cheek but she had to rise on tiptoes to hug him. Unlike Nuray, Cihan was bulky and broad shouldered.

Edom stuck out his head and said hi to Nuray. Then in broken Turkish he said, "*Chok teşekkür*" and thanked her for the food, trying to express his gratitude by speaking her language. Nuray waved her hand a couple of times, indicating that thanks were not needed.

"Okay, Mom, see you. Sleep well, you look tired. You have given us a lot of food, I don't know if we can finish it. And it is heavy." Cihan pretended not to be able to hold the lunch box.

"Come on, you crazy boy! Look at those arms. People will laugh at you if they hear you saying that. When you arrive, call me, okay?"

Raising her voice, she continued: "Don't make excuses like 'There was no signal' or 'My battery died'. Find a way to call me. And zip your coat."

She crossed her arms, fastened her jacket and put her navy blue headband in its place.

"Don't be like Edom. He is American, he has hot blood. People will say are you crazy to go out in that cold. Zip your jacket, come on!"

She stamped her slippers on the floor.

Cihan never understood what his mom meant when she referred to 'people'. Who were those people? If he asked his mom, she would answer, "Who do you think? The strangers". Whenever Nuray began with "If people know" or "If people see", she would keep talking. Cihan felt like the whole world was watching him and their house could be seen from everywhere.

The two young men started their journey.

⋆

Edom was driving while Cihan looked at the maps of the ski center. He was gripping a toothpick between his teeth and spitting out its chips. He pointed to a blue route on the map.

"I think we should go this way."

They had heard there was a snowstorm due that day, but they had already booked the ski center and hotel. It was Friday, and the following Monday was a Memorial Day so they would have an extra day to ski. Cihan had finished his master's thesis and defended it, so he could relax and give himself the Tahoe holiday as a present.

They were following a windy road past the mountains as if following the pleats of a ballerina's skirt in an amusement park, but this was real.

"If the car skids, we're dead. Rannan will strangle me."

"Hahaha, after you're already dead?"

"No time for jokes, Cihan. I only got this car by begging. All his belongings are very valuable to him, you know."

"Why did you borrow it then? We could have gone in your lemon."

"Okay, and then we would be skiing already. Are you crazy? Climb a mountain in a sports car? Think about it, Cihan, nobody would notice we were dead. We would swing through the branches in the car like Tarzan. Tarzan with a car."

He laughed.

"How easily you speak of death, Edom."

"Why do you say that? Do you have a hard time speaking of death?"

"Yes, I'm afraid of death."

"I find it illogical to be afraid of something inevitable."

FIFTEENTH SCENE

"Logic? You look for logic in death?"

"Actually, this is the first time you've said you're afraid of something. You've always been a hero to me: a strong person who does everything best."

"Is it because I run faster than you? I got two bronze medals, but that is not proof of power. Overtaking yourself is the proof of power."

"So?"

"I think the one who isn't afraid of death is the strong one."

"Who?"

"Don't know. Why don't you start the wipers, Edom? It's raining!"

"It's nothing. Last year in Florida I was caught in rain so heavy that you couldn't see beyond the end of your nose. I've told you, right? When we went to inspect to the new chocolate shops with Dad."

"Yes, a hundred times. Don't tempt fate. If we get caught in that much rain at the top of the mountain, we're doomed."

"Don't worry, nothing will happen. Here it doesn't rain that much, it's a tropical climate. What I was talking about was rain both fast and continuous. A curtain of rain falls on the windows of the car and the adrenalin gets crazy high."

"Edi, shut up. Don't you see it *is* getting heavier while you're talking?"

"OMG, really? But it'll be over soon. This kind of rain doesn't last long."

Cihan caught Edom's wrist.

"Don't pull my arm. Hey, you are gonna make me crash, not the rain. How can I go any slower? We won't get anywhere."

"Stop, then!"

"What, on the top of the mountain? Don't yell at me like that! If you know better, you drive!"

The car wobbled off course. Cihan straightened the wheel.

"Okay, Edi. Look forwards, I will shut up now."

"Looking and seeing are not the same thing, Cihan. I look but don't see. I can't help it."

"Understanding and living are also not the same, Edom. You can get it, but cannot live it."

"What do you call that, 'The Philosophy of Water'?"

"No, 'The Fear of Death.'"

SIXTEENTH SCENE

"Hey, Melo, what's wrong with you? You slept through the whole lecture. Are you sick?" asked Nicole, whispering.

Meltem slowly raised her head, shook the hair from in front of her eyes then laid her head back on the table.

"It's nothing."

Nicole was wearing her pink blouse with her green jacket and had left her hair undone. She had put foundation on her freckles which made her look dull.

"Meltem, let's go get a coffee to wake you up. We'll be in the exam soon, you have to get a grip!"

"But I have diarrhea. And nausea."

Meltem pushed herself up and went to the toilet with Nicole. Nicole opened the cold water faucet.

"Come on, wash your face."

Meltem scooped up the water and rinsed her face randomly. Nicole torn down a paper towel and gave it to Meltem.

"What's up with you? Tell me, now!"

"Oh, I had a pill last night, so now my head feels heavy."

"Why? Are you sick? What pill did you have?"

"I don't know!"

"Are you nuts? You cannot take a random pill."

"But all night I was high, as if I was on the clouds. I couldn't sleep, of course. Maybe after four I slept a bit."

"Meltem, you are being stupid."

"Okay, don't come at me. Leave me alone."

Meltem noticed Nicole's nails and changed the subject.

"Let me look—what happened to your nails?" She took Nicole's hand and looked closely at her fingers. "Nicole, you're gonna eat your nail polish anyway, so change the color. The red one looks like blood. Halloween is over!"

Nicole drew her hand away.

"None of your business!"

"Okay then, I'm out of here!"

"Wait a minute, Melo, tell me the name of the pill. I'm curious."

"This girl never forgets anything," mumbled Meltem, shaking her head.

SEVENTEENTH SCENE

Nuray tugged at sweatpants that were too tight for her belly and lifted her blouse up. There was a zigzag line on her belly, another crack added to the many cracks of giving birth. She had gained weight again as she hadn't been following her diet plan for days. She stood in front of the scales in the corner of the room, but was afraid of weighing herself. She didn't want to look at first; she thought if she stood on tiptoes her weight would be less. First she put her toes on the scales, then her whole feet and read what was on the screen.

"Oh, I have reached 89kg."

She felt sad, lost her hope, because she had gained four more kilograms in two weeks. Sadness and stress made her eat whatever she had in the fridge, but now all the things she had been eating began eating her. She lay down on the bed; it had been a long time since she had last rested when she lay down. Changing her head like she changed her clothes would be very good.

*

"Nuray, I'm home!"

Şahin was pale, wearing a pale cream jacket. It was eleven in the morning, but the long maroon curtains were still closed. His mood got gloomier. He left his black case near the door and put his laptop bag on the table, then he opened the curtains.

While he was taking off his jacket a colorful Las Vegas fridge magnet he had bought from the airport dropped out of his pocket. He took it from the ground and looked for the similar Eiffel Tower model. His arm hurt again and he remembered what had happened on the Paris metro. Some pains were remembered through smells, and some through the symbols of places.

Şahin was always hungry after domestic flights in the U.S.A. Eating only two pieces of biscuit made the flights longer; his stomach was grumbling. He opened the door of the fridge and saw his favorite dish: eggplant with meat in it. Şahin couldn't wait to eat it.

"I love this woman," he said, but couldn't even believe himself. Nuray didn't do anything that he didn't approve of, but she wasn't a beautiful woman. She was dark, short and overweight.

*

Nuray was crying in her bed. She wiped her nose on the sheets, then couldn't believe she had done that. Maybe she didn't care anymore. She already knew that Şahin was at home, but still she didn't move. There were noises in the kitchen, probably Şahin slurping from that big bowl of eggplant. He would take a shower after; he had become very sweaty since they got married. Nuray laughed at that as he was always cold too. He even slept with a thick blanket in the summer.

"He must have worn a lot of things not to get cold in the plane, and now he doesn't know how to take them off."

Nuray laughed and cried at the same time. She was very angry at her husband, and even more resentful. However, she still felt sorry for him when he was sweaty and cold. She would embrace her husband as if he was her child; that was the meaning of being a

SEVENTEENTH SCENE

woman and mother. That was what her mom had taught her. Sabahat always advised her to be tidy, neat and patient, and Nuray had programmed herself with these three words: tidiness, neatness and patience. Neither more nor less, and for some irritatingly perfect.

Nuray was thinking about how to express herself. How hard was it to talk to the heart? She put all the things she had been thinking for the past few nights in order.

She would tell him how she knew he was carrying on another relationship, that she had become aware of it six months ago and how she was sure he loved the other woman. She had heard all the conversations he had at midnight on the phone. She had read all the emails filled with love. She was aware that Şahin's hawk-figure lighter was Linda's present, and that they stayed in the same hotel room during business trips as she could smell a woman when she opened his luggage. She would yell at her husband's face that he had a mustache only because Linda wanted him to. He had hated mustaches for years.

She finally gathered her courage and threw the blanket around her, went to the bathroom and looked at her face. She was red-eyed from crying and her face was pale. Her hands were cold. She neatened her flowered pajamas, which were tight again, and she placed a purple satin headband on her head, inhaling deeply. While she was climbing down the stairs, it was also a journey to her inside. The truth she would face hurt her.

When she finally reached her destination, she caught a man eating heartily. That guy was such a stranger to her; he was so far away. The distance was as long as the distance between Turkey and the U.S.A. The emotions were as deep as the Atlantic Ocean between the two countries. One of them was on the surface while the other was in the deepest depths.

What kind of a marriage is this? The roof is in one place and the groundwork is in another. She couldn't say this out loud as she didn't want to make her pain even bigger.

Şahin dropped his food on the table when he saw the expression on his wife's face. He was slurping, just as Nuray had guessed he would be.

"Ah, were you at home?"

His round glasses drooped down his nose and his baldness was more visible when he leaned on the table. He was getting older, like Nuray.

"Why didn't you make a noise? Were you sleeping? Your eyes are red, have you been watching that TV series again? Where are the kids? Won't you say welcome to your husband?"

He opened his arms wide to hug her; to give her his fake love.

Nuray reached her husband and closed her eyes. She put her right hand on the table, preparing to say her memorized words. Şahin was listening; the audience was impatient.

She intended to say, "I want to divorce," but the truth was too heavy. Because hers wasn't the name in the heart of her man, she couldn't say a word. The woman of the house found herself homeless in the man she had thought she was close to, but who was actually very far away.

Her roof collapsed, and so did Nuray. She fainted and her words were spoken to the ground.

EIGHTEENTH SCENE

When Sabahat heard about the cracks in her daughter's marriage, she went to San Francisco and tried to repair the damage in the green house at 69 Turk Street. But she was unsuccessful as the two mainstays of the home had already begun leaving.

Sabahat was short and a little bit overweight, just like an older Nuray, but Sabahat never repressed her emotions like her daughter and granddaughter. She was outspoken.

Şahin had a great respect for his mother-in-law. He was waiting on her hand and foot, portraying himself as a good family guy. Nuray saw these attempts as flattery. The man she had married twenty-five years ago was gone and had been replaced by one the opposite of him.

"Emir, don't spill this plate on the floor. You'll play with the train later. Finish your food and we'll go out. Maybe we'll go to park?"

Emir kicked the table with his feet.

"I don't want to go to the park, I want to go to the aquarium."

Since Emir had been diagnosed with ADHD Nuray had stopped getting angry at him. She accepted her son was hyperactive and kept her patience, even when his desires were irrational

"Okay, honey, we'll go to the aquarium, but let your grandma get a little rest. She just got here last night. Going immediately to the aquarium will not be good for your grandma. She is tired, aren't you, Mom?"

Sabahat was cleaning the jars of jam with wet wipes.

"Nuray, we should cook first."

"Mommy, there is no need to cook. We'll buy something. I think today we should rest."

"Good heavens, why would you buy food? I don't eat food that strangers have made."

"We'll buy some Chinese or Indian. Spicy meat, Mom. If you try it, you'll love it. We all love that kind of food."

"No, I don't eat things I don't know. I only know my country. Let's cook some Turkish food then go out. Otherwise, I'll stay at home."

"Okay, Mom. Whatever you wish."

When Sabahat saw Emir climbing on the fireplace, she began waving.

"Look, Nuray, where he climbed! Come down, boy, you are gonna fall. When did this naughty boy go from here to there?"

Nuray was used to Emir's quickness.

"That's nothing, Mom. We are just grateful that he doesn't climb to the ceiling and swing from the lamps."

"Why don't you put socks on this kid? He is always on the floor, he'll get a stomachache!"

"Don't worry, Mom, he won't!"

"What kind of blood does this strange country have? Everybody on the street wearing nothing on their legs and flip-flops but also jackets. What's the world coming to? Isn't it cold for them? The weather changes from person to person in this American place? The wind is blustering, though, and it's frosty."

EIGHTEENTH SCENE

Sabahat placed the homemade tomato paste in the cupboard. Nuray took it out again, opened the jar and smelled it.

"Mom, I've missed this smell so much!"

"You've always told me that my homemade paste is sour, so actually I brought this for Şahin."

Sabahat kept emptying her food luggage.

"Oh Mom, I love it now. I have even started loving the things I used to hate most: silverberry, mulberry or black grapes. I sometimes buy them here, but their taste is different, Mom. The soil makes them taste different, or maybe it's because once you miss something so much, everything hits home."

Seeing the tear-filled eyes of her daughter, Sabahat also started wiping a little tear away.

"Okay, then. As long as you will eat them, I will send you more. We've cooked a lot of this fresh with the neighbors."

"Mom, I can't believe you!" Nuray saw the pasta. She treated every item coming out of the bag as it was treasure. "The kids will be thrilled by the pasta you have made for us!"

"I stopped by Grandma Şukufe's before coming here. She gave it to me as she knows you love it."

Meltem hugged Sabahat from behind and covered her face with her long dark hair.

"Did somebody say kids? Woooo, pasta, yeah! Let's cook it tonight, please!"

"Pasta? It's not pasta, girl, it's *makarna*. Check your eyesight."

"But Grandma, here it is called pasta."

"Nuray, unzip that bag. Yes, there is a black plastic bag wrapped around white towels. There is flatbread with meat in it inside. I was going to throw it in the freezer to eat later, but I forgot in the excitement."

"It's okay, Mother, then our dinner is already ready. Let's go!"

"You're great, Grandma! It's great you are here! What should I say in Turkish, Mom? *Evimiz şeşelendi?*"

"It's not that, Meltem!" Nuray opened the door of the fridge.

"Anyway, I tried." Meltem kissed her grandmother on the cheek.

"Where is Cihan, Meltem?"

"Playing basketball in the garden."

"Tell him to get ready. He can give us a ride after we have eaten something."

The door to the garden opened and Cihan came into the house, wiping his face on his wet blue shirt, and went up the stairs. The sound of the water could be heard from the second floor bathroom as he took a shower, competing with the sound of the cutlery in the kitchen.

Cihan came downstairs, fragrant with aftershave. When he opened the door to his car, he smiled at the three women and a little naughty kid who were waiting for him.

When he turned the radio on, his mother warned him immediately, "Turn down the volume, Cihan!"

*

Sabahat asked, "So this is the place you said is famous?"

"Yes, Grandma, don't you like it here? Hey, look at these sea lions!"

"No, I like it, but I don't know—it seems like it doesn't have many things."

Everybody complained about Sabahat's pickiness. She always found something she didn't like, as if she tried to find excuses not to like anything.

EIGHTEENTH SCENE

Wearing black pants, bone-colored shirt, black boots and a ponytail, Meltem looked like she was going to a job interview rather than on an outing.

"You're here for maybe the thousandth time and you still take photos? I can't believe you, Meltem."

"Don't stick your nose in, Cihan, just take my photo. No comment. It is hard to capture the right light—don't you know? I don't keep all of them anyway, just the beautiful ones."

"Okay, okay, pretend I didn't say anything."

"Just get my face in the frame and focus on the view, right?"

"Look, I never take a good photo!"

"Okay, just shoot it. I'll crop and fix it later."

"But you can't make your straight hair curly, hahaha!"

"Do not worry, I will be able to soon!"

"What? A camera that makes ugly beautiful?"

"Mom, did you hear what Cihan said?"

"Cihan, stop making fun of the girl, at least when we're with your grandma! Don't act like children. Look at Emir, does he make any sound?"

"Mom, I have to pee!"

"I told you to go to the bathroom before we left the house."

"I didn't have to go then, but now I do, Mom."

"We've just arrived here, Emir, isn't that too soon?"

"What am I doing here? One of you has to pee while the other keeps taking photos. I'm bored, you have fun!" Cihan combed his hair back with his fingers.

"Nuray, tell Meltem to take photos later. You're always here anyway. Look, the kid insists on going to aquarium, so let's go there first. I should let you know I may not be able to walk a lot as my knees are already hurting."

Sabahat rubbed her knees.

"Okay, Mommy, it's close, right at the back."

"Mom, carousel!"

"Don't you have to pee?"

"Now it's gone. Look, look, I don't need to pee! Let's ride the carousel!"

NINETEENTH SCENE

Reb dialed the last number she had promised to call: (415)-723-18...

"Hello! This is Streetlight, how can I help you?"

"Well, my six-year-old daughter and I want to come and stay. Do you have any beds?"

"Wait a minute, please!"

Reb waited.

"Your name, please?"

"It's Reb, sir, R-E-B."

"Well, er, Reb, unfortunately we don't have any beds. Please keep on calling because every day a few beds become vacant, but for now we have none. I'm sorry."

"This is the last shelter I've called. Please help me! I've stayed at the airport with my daughter for the past two days."

"Wait, I'll dial you through to the director."

Biiip biiiip!

"Ma'am, we would like to help you, but we can't promise a bed. You had better come here—is that all right?"

"Thanks, you're amazing. Thanks a lot, you've made my day!"

★

Reb and Mariana got off the bus on 17th Street and began walking. They were climbing up a hill, the hill of their lives. It was hard to walk on as it was too steep for them, climbing their lives while still being thankful to be alive. Mariana tied up her hair with strawberry ribbons; she was wearing a green raincoat with pink butterflies and rain boots and pulling her toy luggage, sniffing. Reb was walking along in her brown furry coat, black boots and a messy bun. She still didn't want to believe that they were now homeless.

"Mom, where are we going now?"

"I told you, we'll stay with others at a guesthouse till we find a new home."

"I don't want to stay with others, Mom."

"Think what fun it will be. Maybe you'll find a new friend there."

"All my friends are at school, Mom. I don't want a new friend."

"I guess you will need to enroll in a new school. You know, this place will be too far from your school—if we get accepted—so it will be hard to go there every day. So, you will go to the same school as the other kids there."

"No, I don't like that place!"

"You haven't seen it, maybe you'll love it."

"I don't think so."

Mariana closed her eyes, which meant she didn't want to listen anymore. Reb didn't insist on carrying on the conversation. Instead she opened a water bottle and drank a little, then asked if her daughter wanted to drink.

"No."

"Okay, Mariana, don't push it so much! You could pretend to like this place for a short while, couldn't you?"

Reb tried to emphasize that it was she who made the decisions and Mariana had to help her. She didn't want to tell Mariana that

NINETEENTH SCENE

they had no other choice. She found their homelessness weird indeed. She felt like they were in a nightmare they couldn't escape from.

"How much longer do we have to walk?"

"Just a little more."

"How much exactly? For example, if we use the rug in my room as a measurement, how many rugs do we have to pass? Or how many Bos?"

"I don't know. That's a strange measurement."

"Please, guess!"

"Bo is so small, how much room could he take up in the world?"

"Not really, he is as long as my two feet, Mom. But when I stand up I fill as much space as Bo. If we put our footprints over each other, they would be seen as one. We are actually very small, aren't we, Mom."

*

When they arrived at the shelter, a fat double-chinned woman with a peeping voice welcomed them. She repeated that there were no places. When Reb told her that she had talked with the director on the phone and she had told them to come, the woman called someone and talked to them slowly. When she lowered her peeping voice, it became childish.

After a while a tall masculine woman came into the room. She was wearing high-waisted navy-blue pants and a cream and blue striped shirt.

"You are the one I talked to on the phone, right?" She spoke very slowly. "Follow me. We'll go right to the end of the corridor."

"Mom, what is this place? Who is this man?"

"I told you, this is the guesthouse, and this *lady* is the director."

"She is a she? But she looks like a he."

"Shh, Mariana, be quiet. They will throw us out if you keep on like that."

"This is the place where you'll sleep. We've put emergency beds in the laundry room, and you can stay if you want. I'm sorry that the big bedroom is full, but I couldn't reject you because of the young lady. I should inform you this bed will become unavailable soon, so you should decide immediately. If any bed goes vacant, I'll inform you. Families with children have priority."

Reb thought it was more convenient than the street and quickly said, "We accept, ma'am, even if it is temporary. Thanks."

"Okay, I'll send you your bed."

The dirty laundry smelled very bad. There were four washing machines and two dryers in the room.

"Mom, this place is even smaller than our bathroom."

Reb crouched down. Face to face with her daughter, she squeezed her shoulders.

"Darling, we have to stay in here until the other beds are vacant. I'm sorry for this, but I promise you I'll fix it as soon as possible. Trust me, okay?"

Mariana wanted to trust her mom, but it was hard, especially in a situation like this. She was very sad because she'd had to leave her pink-flowered strawberry-scented blanket behind and sleep on a dirty mattress on the floor of a laundry room.

A blond woman came in and gave a mattress to Reb.

"This is yours. I could find only one pillow and you'll have to share the blanket."

Reb was thankful that she wasn't fat as she and Mariana both had to sleep on a mattress that was even too small for her. At least they had a roof over their heads. Reb dressed her daughter in the

NINETEENTH SCENE

princess pajamas she had taken from her luggage then kissed her on the cheek.

"Go to sleep, my beautiful princess. Tomorrow will be better."

"Mom, where are you gonna sleep?"

"Next to you."

"But it is too small for you to fit."

"I'll fit, look!"

Reb lay down beside Mariana. She almost fell off the mattress, her hip was touching the ground, but she smiled with the strength of motherhood. They were face to face, looking at each other sadly. They couldn't hide their sorrow from each other.

Reb switched off the lights as it was past twelve. A woman came into the room. She was short, thin, petite—a bag of bones, indeed. She filled the machines from the bag of laundry she had then put some detergent in them.

"No, this can't be happening. You won't start the machine now, will you?"

"Of course I will. They will need to wear the clothes in the morning. I won't disturb you to put them in the dryer as long as you do it after the washing is finished."

"But how will we possibly sleep through this noise?"

"I don't know, but there are lots of people waiting for these clothes and they don't have furry coats like you!"

Reb was glad that Mariana was already asleep, but it was impossible for her to do the same. Furry coat? Why did the thin woman mention her furry coat? When did she see it? She must have wanted to imply Reb was rich.

Reb finally fell asleep after four when she had put the laundry in the dryer.

Mariana woke up. When she saw her mother was sleeping, she took out the cell phone Reb had hidden in her sock. She found Mirza's number and wrote an SMS for him.

Mirza, we don't have a home anymore.

Her mother moved a little, and Mariana deleted the message she had sent and put the phone back in its place.

Reb woke when the homeless came to take their clothes and woke Mariana up immediately. Mariana wanted to sleep a little bit more, but they had to leave. When the sun came up, everybody had to go, so Reb swallowed her tears inside and made Mariana stand up. When she had gone to school she had been the same, but back then Reb had laughed at her innocent begging.

Reb and Mariana went out and walked to the nearest park. Reb sat on a bench and Mariana put her head on her lap. Reb covered her daughter with her coat. The sun wasn't shining yet, only winking at the day and slowly rising in the sky.

Reb took out her phone and saw the SMS that Mirza had sent.

Where are you?

And then another one.

Give me your location, I'm waiting.

"What was that about?" she said and turned off her phone. A voice inside her said that Mirza could save them. Just because he was in a wheelchair didn't mean that he wasn't able to do anything. She got angry at that idea. It was the ones who walked who didn't do anything for them.

TWENTIETH SCENE

Mariana and Reb stayed in the park all day after their sleepless night. For the first time ever, Mariana didn't want to play in the park. Playing was only fun if there was a home to go to after, otherwise even playing was senseless. Mariana got bored of playing and sat on the sidewalk, suddenly beginning to scratch. She was itching all over.

Reb realized Mariana was suffering and sat next to her. She examined Mariana's hair and saw little black things. Reb didn't know how to get rid of them; she had never seen them in her life before. She got angry, felt sorry for herself, but she had no choice. She couldn't quit being a mother so she laid Mariana over her knees. That was when she understood the real difficulties of being a mother.

*

Reb and Mariana joined the food line at the Streetlight that evening.

"You go to that table in front of the wall. I'll fetch the meal and come straight over."

"No, I want to go with you."

"Okay, your choice."

Reb was exhausted, but she had this small girl with her, and Mariana was all she had. Once a small girl herself, now Reb had to cope with everything alone.

"Mom, look! Look, Mom!" Mariana began hitting her knees. "He's the man."

Mariana hid behind her mom.

"Which man? I don't know what you mean."

Mariana was screaming and now everyone was looking in the direction she was pointing. Reb tried to look and protect her daughter at the same time, and all she saw was a man with a white baseball hat and a surprised face. She couldn't see his eyes so she didn't know who he was.

Mariana's feet were in the air. She held onto her mother's neck like an octopus.

"Is there a problem?" A big-breasted black woman came over to them. Reb couldn't help thinking that she was showing too much cleavage.

"No, ma'am, she'll stop soon. I apologize."

"Okay, get her to stop immediately."

A man behind them with only three strands of white hair was shaking his arms like a puppet.

"I'll take food as the young girl is crying."

"Okay, you take it, sir."

"I'll take food as the young girl is crying."

"I told you it was okay, sir, go ahead."

"I'll take…"

The man continued over and over, and Reb finally realized he was sick and couldn't help himself.

"I took, I took, I took…"

TWENTIETH SCENE

He was now repeating this over and over, but in a low voice.

"Mariana, I cannot carry you anymore. Look, it's our turn to take some food. How can I possibly carry the food tray while holding you? We'll both fall over."

Reb whispered into her daughter's ears and kissed away her tears. She tasted the saltiness of Mariana's pain, the most difficult part of being a mother. She could handle Mariana's tears and whims as she was her mother, but with all eyes upon her, she became defenseless. Whatever she did would be seen as a fault. Maybe others would have calmed Mariana down differently; maybe they would have yelled at her. Everything was possible for the others, but it was she who had to decide and perform the mothering she knew.

"No, please don't leave me. I cannot stay in the same place as a thief, he may also steal us."

Mariana's lips were shaking. Reb was already carrying all her sorrow, and now she had to carry her six-year-old daughter. All day they had played in the park and picked flowers. She had tried to keep Mariana distracted by saying a wonderful meal would be waiting for them in the evening. She had to do this as she was penniless and couldn't buy food throughout the day. She was very hungry too, but her maternal instinct made her ignore that.

They left the food line and sat at the first table they saw empty, turning their backs on the man in the white hat. They were scared of him. So many strange things were happening to them, and this man was the king of the strangeness.

Mariana put her head on her mother's shoulder. A hand reached round from behind them. Mariana screamed, but her scream wasn't caused by fear but happiness.

Reb couldn't believe her eyes. It was Bo.

"I'm sorry, young lady, please forgive me. I didn't know we lived in the same home. Look, I kept him for you."

"Bo, my only friend, I've missed you so much!"

Mariana was hugging her teddy bear, but she didn't look at Johnson's face. She was very angry with him, but against all the odds, she was happy. Bo made her forget her homelessness; she was only a child again.

Reb would never have thought Mariana would snatch Bo this way. What kind of revenge was that? Had this guy cursed them?

Unexpectedly Reb asked the homeless man to sit with them.

The African American man with the blue eyes and the white hat turned his head, put his hand on his heart and asked "Me?" as if ashamed.

Reb suddenly felt some affection for the guy from the bus, even though she too had been very angry with him. She answered his question with a nod of her head. Johnson turned the chair behind him round and sat beside them. He crossed his arms and put his head on them, looking very innocent. Reb forgot about her own homelessness then and felt sorry for him.

"Hi, I'm Johnson. Nice to meet you."

"I'll forgive you for taking Bo on one condition." Reb pointed her index finger at him.

"What's that?"

"Why you are here? Why you are a homeless? Tell us."

"Why I am homeless? It's a simple question but very hard to answer. It's strange, I've never told anybody this story."

"And?"

"I'll redeem myself. Listen."

TWENTY-FIRST SCENE

Forty-five, forty-six, forty-seven...sixty. It was done. She had counted to sixty twice so it must have been two minutes. She was about to look at the stick in her hand, but stopped. She didn't have the courage. She tried looking at the stick from a distance; she didn't know whether she was ready to face the truth. Putting some lavender scented soap into her palm, she washed her hands. Finally she took a deep breath, closed her eyes, dried her hands and took the stick, opening her eyes again.

There was a smiling baby on the screen. She didn't know whether to laugh or cry. She wanted to scream in joy and anger. Was it nice to have a life growing inside her body? She hadn't even got used to her own life, how she could carry a child's?

But there was a life in her, and it was real. She had two hearts now; it was exciting. Not the same person as her, but a piece of her; not exactly a piece of her, but attached to her, tied to her internally.

"She will be my baby soon. My God, I'll be a mother."

She wrapped the pregnancy test in toilet paper and threw it in the garbage, then took out her phone and called someone.

*

"Linda, what are you talking about? A baby? I've already got three kids. I hope you're not thinking about having it. No, you won't do that to me, will you?"

"I only...I thought you'd be happy..."

"Happy? Linda, are you crazy? You know I'm married. If my wife hears about this, my marriage is over. I think it is time for you and I to break up."

Linda heard two lots of bad news at the same time and words mumbled in her mouth. She wanted to hurt him, but she couldn't do it. She wanted to curse him, but the words hid like a small child hiding behind her mother's back. Instead, she tried one more time with nice words.

"Break up? I love you, Şahin, and I want to have this kid. Let's talk it over."

"There is nothing to talk about. If you want to have this baby it means you don't want me. If you love me, you'll prove it by making this baby disappear."

"How can you say that? This is your child, not an ugly, ugly word."

"*Hadi, haaaaaadi...*"

"What? What's *Haaaaadiii*?" asked Linda, but he had hung up the phone.

Linda didn't understand anything. She hadn't expected such a bad reaction. Şahin had known they were having unprotected sex, so she just couldn't get his attitude. Their relationship's fate hung on an abortion. Linda had to make a choice, a very hard one. It was a huge gift for her to have fallen pregnant before she turned forty. What Şahin was telling her to give up was a lifetime of motherhood. She could give up most anything, but giving up on motherhood would mean crushing herself.

Therefore there was only one option.

*

While Meltem was filling her car with gas, her phone rang. A woman wearing clown makeup was on the screen.

"Hi, Nicole!"

"Where are you, Meltem?"

Nicole was talking as if the phone was in her mouth, her voice charged with excitement.

"I'm here, where are you?"

"Stop joking, I need to talk to you immediately."

"Okay. I'm at the gas station now, but I'll be home in half an hour. Come round. My grandma is staying with us, but whatever we will talk in my room."

*

Nicole knocked at the door as if she wanted to break it. Nuray hurried to open it, surprised when she saw Nicole.

"Isn't Meltem at home, Nuray?"

"No, but she will be here any minute."

"Yes, we've just talked on the phone. Can I wait in her room?"

Nicole rushed up the stairs. Sabahat complained from the kitchen table.

"Why are you mumbling? I cannot hear you."

Nuray carried on rounding the potato meatball in her hand.

"What can I say? These foreigners are so free and comfortable. She just ran up to Meltem's room. No respect at all. And she called you Nuray, did I hear correctly? You're not her friend, though."

"Mom, Nicole is like our daughter. She's Meltem's best friend. You know foreigners don't call adults Uncle or Aunt. They call everyone by their names."

"Your home is such a common place. Edom is your son as well? He was here all the time when I was here last."

Sabahat held onto her kerchief. She always wore it in the kitchen as she didn't want her hair to get in the meals. She also advised Nuray to wear one, but Nuray was already wearing colorful headbands.

The door opened: it was Meltem, who asked if Nicole had arrived. The two women at the table pointed to the stairs and Meltem ran up to her room.

Nuray was very curious.

"Mom, why don't we bake a cake for teatime?"

"I don't want to, Nuray. I have high blood sugar, no cake for me."

"But the kids will eat it, Mom. I will bake it in a minute."

She took the eggs out of the fridge.

"I know your intentions, girl. Okay, do it and feed your curiosity."

Nuray put the slices of cake on a plate. It was still hot and her little finger got burned, but she just sucked it to lessen the pain. She didn't even spare time to run it under cold water. She couldn't wait much longer; she had to learn what was going on upstairs.

She knocked at the door to Meltem's room three times: *tak, tak, tak!*

TWENTY-SECOND SCENE

She let her long, dark hair flow down over her shoulders and blue eye-makeup flashed from her dark-brown eyes. She was wearing a black turtleneck jumper and jeans, and creeping to the place she wanted to go.

When she finally got there, she began looking around like a scared kitty. She locked her eyes onto the ceiling of San Francisco State University café, only just realizing that the roof was so high. The place seemed to be getting bigger while she was getting smaller.

Sadaf bit her lip and painted a fake smile on her face. She drank hot coffee from her mug, but she was cold inside. Sadaf was becoming less and less, taken over by her soul. When the ice melted, the flood would come and she was afraid of that.

She pulled at the sleeves of her jumper. Her classmate from Jordan, Muna, looked at her from head to toe while adjusting her white headscarf. She saw Sadaf's pain but couldn't say anything.

When Sadaf had first mentioned not wearing her headscarf to her mother, she had realized it was herself who she was actually trying to convince.

"I don't know, Mom. A voice inside me tied me up to a chair. I have to listen to it, otherwise it will execute me."

"For what?"

"The voice inside me controls me like a government and forces me to be free."

"How come a voice governs you, Sadaf? What do you mean?"

"You know in Iran women were forced to wear headscarves because of government and social oppression? The opposite is happening in me."

"Then don't you need to resist this oppression? Who else can control a body possessed by you?"

"Mom, the power inside you is always stronger than the power on the outside. Whatever it says will happen."

"Will you be happy?"

"I don't know. I'm not doing this to be happy. I'm gonna do it because I cannot resist. Also I've never tried it. I want to see myself in that way. I want to meet that Sadaf."

"Why, though?"

"I'm at a loose end. The voices in me are clapping and cheering for me to be free. I feel like my headscarf is my disability. When I wear it, I cannot walk properly. The headscarf gets in my way."

"How is that possible? It is on your head," said Umah.

"I don't know either. This is something I couldn't solve."

"Then you must walk upside-down. Walk with your head and force your feet to think. What you call knowledge is you, Sadaf. When you finally give in to this government oppression, you'll find yourself in prison and want the opposite. You can never escape from your conscience, dear."

"You don't know what Natalie told me. She said I have never experienced the wind in my hair or my hair blowing across my lips. I have never carried my beauty on the street, only hidden it from strangers. I told her that I was happy, but how could I know without trying? You may laugh at me, but I want to give it a try. I'm content with my life, I was raised like that, but I want to see if I'm missing something. It's not nonsense, is it? Don't judge me, I have lots of questions in my mind. Mom, I need a change."

"Sadaf, this is your life. I have no right to tell you what to do. The decision is yours. However, I want you to know that you can only be free as long as you become one with your soul. This owner of you knows better than you how you can be free and happy. Your body is only given to you for a short time."

*

Sadaf sat in the café all day. She drank four cups of coffee then went outside to smoke. She had always hated the smell of smoking, but she was trying all the things she had never tried. It was cold, but she was shivering more because of the fire inside her. Her hair was touching her cheeks.

She waited next to a streetlamp in her velvet hat and red scarf, thinking about her actions that day. She hadn't covered her head, but she had hidden herself from the outside. Actually, the only change in her clothes was not covering her head, but she felt naked and she had never thought she would feel that way. She felt like she was without a roof.

She laughed at herself as she wasn't even able to smoke. She put out the cigarette and walked toward the train station. On the way she saw homeless people and realized she too was homeless without her cover. Her hat wasn't enough to hold her mind in its place. That morning while checking herself in the mirror she had seemed very pretty with her makeup and dark wavy hair, but now that beautiful hair had become arrows, hurting her mind. She felt the same pain as she had when she'd pulled her wisdom teeth out.

The view looked like one of the small paintings in the corner of a big art gallery. A girl was standing in the train station with a black hat and red scarf. It was a painting of loneliness which drew the attention of no one. Sadaf wondered whether there would be anyone besides her in the next station or whether she would stay lonely all her life.

She took off her hat, wanting to feel the wind, but the wind was strong and made her hair whip her face. Things didn't feel the way she'd hoped. She wanted to know when the feeling of homelessness would go away.

"The cover is your home, and it shows your beauty," Sadaf realized at the end of the day. All day she'd felt as if everything, even inanimate objects, was watching her. She had never looked at herself in this way and she was uncomfortable with the feeling. Everybody had become a mirror for her, and it was a painful experience.

*

Sadaf checked the mailbox before entering her home. There was an insurance company advertisement, some credit card invoices and a tourism catalogue.

"Oh, there are discount tours to heaven!"

Her face fell as she felt as if she was in hell, and she needed to get rid of that feeling. She was feeling sick from the peppermint gum she had put in her mouth after smoking. As she looked for her keys to enter the flat, the mail fell down on the ground. She bent down to pick it up, and at that moment the door opened.

"Ah, Sadaf."

Lara immediately showed off her new lilac dress, twirling around.

"How do I look?"

She struck a pose, then realized something was different.

"Sadaf, you've forgotten something! I knew you had been thinking about it, but..."

TWENTY-SECOND SCENE

Sadaf ran directly to her room. Lara ignored her. She had her own problems. The dress on her was three hundred dollars, but she liked it anyway and she didn't like returning the things she bought. As a result she had many clothes in her wardrobe that had never been worn.

Lara took a shower, and was drying her hair in the bathroom when Sadaf walked in as the door was open. Lara stopped the hair dryer and winked at her.

"You'll get used to it, Sadaf. This is only your first day. You should live whatever way you're happy."

Sadaf already knew how she would become happy again. She took her veil and apologized, saying: "This is the period that completes a woman's beauty sentence. If there is no period, you can't stop."

Angel Island: The Building of the Heart's Eye

Lara was walking in the tunnels of her soul. It was just as easy to open her eyes and see outside, but she wanted to see inside. To achieve her goal, she had entered the building of her heart's eye.

There were all kinds of eyes—small or big, slanted, blue, green, hazel or brown—running around. Their eyelashes had become feet, making them move very fast and open a lot of doors.

She rose up the walls of her soul. On the second floor everything was touch-operated. Not a single thing that had been on the first floor was there; it was a whole new world.

The eyes didn't talk to each other; they only saw what was happening. To cool down a little bit, they opened and closed their eyelids. On a cloud, floating around, they went through the motions. They knew that running would carry Lara higher in the building of her heart so they would be closer to the peaceful lands. They wouldn't get tired till they stopped. The eyes saw their secrets by running, and treasure was opened before them. They found the things they had lost and ran again to give thanks.

There were some eyes neither running nor walking. They only waited in front of the doors, never trying them. Touching the doors might have opened them, but they didn't think to touch them. Their eyelashes were frozen and so were their looks. The sealed eyes were struggling in the one way corridors to have a look. They were losers, and not eyes anymore. They had become sculptures, locked up and sealed in the end.

That was the reason why the eyes that could see and those that couldn't never got on well.

TWENTY-THIRD SCENE

"Hi, you must be in trouble."
Johnson was swaying from side to side, his hands in his pockets like a shy child. Lara wanted to be sure she had not been followed. Her eyes scanned the surroundings, but there was no one around. She shook the dust off her clothes.

"I was kicked out of the park."

Johnson was trying to figure out a solution.

"Why were you kicked out? Where were you sleeping? Wait, you don't seem homeless. Am I wrong?"

Lara felt comfortable as if she was talking to a friend.

"Well, no."

Johnson turned his back and started walking. Lara had no choice but to follow him. After they had walked two blocks, he stopped. Johnson knew Lara was following him even though he hadn't looked back.

He pointed at two Victorian houses. One was white and the other was yellow.

"You can sleep here if you want."

He showed her the dark narrow space between the two houses, just in front of the dog house.

"Here? No way."

"Joe is a good dog. I sometimes put my head inside the house when it is raining. Not a bad place. The weather is nice now, but maybe it will rain at night. You can sleep there and I'll be just in the entrance."

He lay down on the ground abruptly, almost as if he had fallen.

Lara didn't know what to do. She was under the stars between two houses. The street was full of emptiness, and she had no idea how she could handle extra emptiness. Would she ever be full again? She had stupid questions in her mind. It was three in the morning; the streets now belonged to their rightful owners: the homeless. The wind was blowing along the empty street and there were some other noises: dogs, cars and sirens in the distance.

Lara realized that declining Johnson's offer was not an option. She was only a guest on the street and it would be rude to be choosy. She was supposed to be grateful for what she had: a homeless guardian, a dog and a dog house.

Johnson had closed off the entrance to the street. Lara lay down on torn cardboard in front of the dog house. She didn't even remove her boots.

Sleeping was an escape if done under a roof. However, sleeping on the street brought a whole load of troubles. Lara realized what it was like to be on the street in need of sleep. Her body and mind were tired, but the night was eager to race toward morning. Lara put up her black hood and hid her face from the night. The night saw everything the broad daylight saw, but it hadn't told her anything yet.

*

Johnson opened his eyes at 5.30 a.m. He covered his beautiful guest with his jacket and doubled back toward the toilet in Buena Vista Park. He always washed his clothes there, but he hadn't washed himself for two weeks and he smelled very bad. He didn't want Lara to treat him like a street dog, though. He would smell nice to her, only her. The rest of the world knew that he was dirty.

If he was lucky he would finish his job before six. Otherwise, the witch would come and reprimand him. The liquid soap was almost finished so he added some water to it. It was not much, but its smell was enough for him: the smell of cleanliness.

He washed his green T-shirt and black boxers, then put his clothes on the hand dryer machine and his head under the faucet. The water was very cold, and he said, "Ah!" His "Ah!" burst out of him as if his soul would destroy itself. He washed his head under cold water in the morning black frost of San Francisco, then took some paper towels a few at a time. Some fell to the ground, but he also used them. Even his cleaning ritual was dirty. However many times he washed himself his body wasn't going to get clean anyway.

He put his head under the hand dryer to dry his hair; he was tall so he had to lean and his legs ached. Getting clean was a nightmare for him. The door opened and the park janitor entered: a short African-American woman. Normally she cursed whenever she saw him, but this time she just ignored Johnson. She was like a robot without any emotions. Every day at six she came to the toilets to clean them.

Johnson locked himself one of the toilets.

The woman complained when she saw Johnson's clothes.

"You turn the public bathroom into a personal one, you dirt bag."

Johnson usually went to the laundry, but he had no time that day. He had to get back to Lara. He opened the faucet and washed his armpits. His hair was still damp, but he had to hurry back to get approval from a beautiful pair of eyes.

★

TWENTY-THIRD SCENE

Lara opened her eyes and blew the ladybug walking on her hand away. Her boots had become heavier overnight. Her whole body was sore. She stood up and left the jacket on the dog house; she didn't know whose jacket it was. She thought about going back to the park to see if her notebook was still there—she could have been writing the whole night if it hadn't been for that guy—but she decided not to go as the guy might still be there. She would walk to her car instead and go to her home, make some coffee and write about her fear and excitement.

She would throw her clothes in the garbage as they would remind her of the street. They were old and dirty, and a smell that would never wear off was all over them. She had always been attractive with her long wavy hair and high heels, but now she was a tomboy. She had lost her charm; she was ugly. For her being beautiful meant being well-groomed. A beautiful person might be beautiful even in a sack, but that beauty would be without charm.

*

Johnson turned the corner and realized his guest had already left. He was hurt and his eyes filled with tears. His efforts had only been for the eyes of a beautiful woman, but he had lost out. He got mad at himself again.

*

Lara took a warm shower and lay down on the sofa with her wet hair, pink robe and bunny slippers. While eating an apple, she looked through a fashion magazine. The door opened and she jumped from her place.

"Who is it?"

When she saw who it was she sat down again.

"Oh, it is you, Sadaf."

"Yes, why are you so scared of me?"

Lara hadn't told anybody about her plans for the day before as she hadn't wanted them to persuade her not to go. She didn't know how to tell Sadaf now, so she was playing for time by reading the magazine. She took another bite from the apple.

"Where were you last night? I was worried about you, why didn't you tell me that you weren't coming home?"

"I was on the street."

"What do you mean? Were you at a night club?"

"No, I slept on the street where a homeless guy was sleeping. Actually, I was in a dog house."

She realized anew what she had been through. She hadn't been able to comprehend the fear and anxiety while still living it; it had happened too fast, but had taken a lot out of her.

Sadaf got mad at Lara telling it as if it happened every day of her life. She snatched the magazine and threw it on the table.

"What?"

"Nothing bad happened. It was only for observation."

"How? Why? For what observation?"

"Sadaf, please calm down. Let's order a pizza, I'm starving. Then I will tell you everything, I promise."

She laughed as she wanted to change the subject.

"There is no need for pizza. I've cooked biryani, lots of. Taste it, it's not very hot this time."

Sadaf calmed down a little bit, a feeling of kindness filling her.

"Thanks, but I want to have pizza. If you don't, I'm calling the pizza guy."

"Okay, I'll call." She shook her finger at Lara and said, "Don't go anywhere until you've told me everything in detail."

TWENTY-THIRD SCENE

Lara stood up to throw away the apple core. She liked herself after a bath: her cheeks became rosy and her face glowed. Yet she was sure she would like her every other self after that night. And she would know the value of every day.

*

Hi, Yasemin,

I cannot get to sleep, it's 2.37 at night.

These days I am in too deep, please give me a hand. Now what I will tell you may make you say "You're crazy!" I give you the right to say it.

I want somebody to stop me. I want a limit to my freedom in this city with limitless freedom. I'm afraid, maybe because I can do anything I think of and nothing will stop me. There must be something that's wrong someplace, I'm bordering on limitlessness. It could find me any moment.

I kept getting lost. It was ridiculous, completely ridiculous. I should have stopped and looked at the street, then I wouldn't have got lost. Then I would have been able to value my loneliness. "I walked all night and slept all day," I would say when they found me. They would shake me off and all the things on me would settle onto them. I would destroy the city then beg to be forgiven. I would give my reasons: there was no one around to stop me, and I couldn't stop myself. Don't ask me why.

I've lost my name, Yasemin. I don't know myself anymore. I went beyond the ordinary. This city tells me, "You can do whatever you wish." This makes me unhappy. I just stand there and get stuck.

Remind me who I am, and more importantly who I was.

With love,

Anonymous.

TWENTY-FOURTH SCENE

"Hello?"

"Oh, finally! Rebecca, I've been trying to call you since last night. I got a message from you, but don't understand what is happening. Where are you?"

"You can call me Reb."

Reb began crying. When Mariana moved a little while sleeping on her lap, she wiped her nose on her sleeve.

"Well, we...I can't talk right now. Mariana must have sent that message, I had no idea!"

"Okay, okay. Just tell me where you are," said Mirza.

"We are in a park."

"At this hour? It's half past six!"

"Yes, we don't have a home anymore."

"What happened? Never mind, just give me the name of the park. I'll come to pick you up."

"I don't know its name. There is a McDonalds on the right, then a Starbucks on the corner."

"Even in this situation, you joke, Rebecca?"

"I'm not joking."

"In every street, there is a McDonalds and Starbucks. How I am supposed to find you?"

TWENTY-FOURTH SCENE

"Okay, let me think a little. We stayed at Streetlight Homeless Shelter last night and walked from there. We must be not very far away."

"Got it. Don't move anywhere. I'm on my way!"

"We have nowhere to go anyway. We're here."

*

A man in a wheelchair and his driver were looking around so Reb waved at them. Mirza approached Reb and was surprised to see Mariana on her lap, sleeping.

Without asking anything, he said, "We're going home."

"No, I can't."

She lowered her hat over her eyes.

"Mom, please, I don't like that guesthouse."

"Were you listening to us, bad girl? You sent a message to Mirza without asking me, we'll talk that later!"

"Don't get angry with her. She was right. Decide and we'll go immediately."

"I think they'll give us a bed tonight. If we leave now, we won't get one again."

"Reb, you won't come here again. You'll stay with us, I'll talk to my mother."

Mariana hugged Mirza happily and insisted on going.

"Please, Mom."

"Okay, you go tonight and I'll come tomorrow."

"What do you think, Mariana? If you come with us, Umah will cook you naan. You'll love it. And your mother will come tomorrow."

"No, I don't want to leave her alone here."

"Okay, okay, I'll come with you."

Reb couldn't leave her daughter. This offer was a miracle. Reb was both angry and thankful for Mariana sending that message without her knowledge.

★

Reb was sitting at a table filled with hot food in a white high-ceilinged house on Taylor Street. Umah had cooked chicken tikka masala for her guests, and Reb was very hungry so began eating the chicken right away. The sauce spilled on her napkin.

Umah was a tall woman with thick henna-colored hair. She was wearing a white shirt and skirt and had put her hair up in a bun. The tablecloth was all white and the food was served with love. Reb had never been hosted with that much love.

Mirza was watching them. Reb saw she was being watched from behind his glass while he was drinking water. His teeth were pearl white. Reb felt shy and tried to hide it by asking for salt.

After dessert, the dinner was over.

"I'll show you to your room." Umah had prepared a room with two single beds. Reb thought about the laundry room they had stayed in the night before; everything was changing so fast. Her life was at rock bottom yesterday and now it was on the peak; her lifelines were becoming zigzags. She was sure it would go to the bottom again, it was a fact of life, but she wasn't worried about tomorrow.

Umah asked if Reb would mind her giving Mariana a bath. Umah was acting like Mariana's grandma, playing in the bathtub with her. Reb could hear Mariana's laugh and it hit the spot after having heard her weeping. The happiness got bigger, just like the bubbles in the bath.

As Reb was watching them play, Mirza was watching Reb.

TWENTY-FOURTH SCENE

"Reb, would you come into the living room? Let's talk a little."

Reb walked into the room and sat opposite Mirza. She told him everything: how she had been fired and couldn't pay the rent, so she'd had to give up her car and leave her home.

"Why didn't you call me?"

He was angry at her, but mostly he was hurt. They were not very close, but they knew each other more or less.

"Before losing your home, you could have told me. Then maybe you wouldn't have had to leave."

"It happened anyway. I was too shy, I thought you might get me wrong."

Mirza was the wheelchair-bound owner of the pizza house opposite the Dolphin Restaurant. He was a dark, plain man with dark eyes and a stubbly beard, the treasured only son of a rich Pakistani family. One afternoon, Mariana had insisted on cheese pizza and they had gone to Mirza's restaurant together. Mirza had been very lovely to her and her daughter, and once in a while, when Mariana visited her workplace, Reb would let her to go to Mirza and play.

Reb knew that Mirza liked her, but she didn't want to give him any hope. She was about to tell him that, but the fire in the fireplace stopped her. The words would burn out when there was love involved.

"Don't worry. You can stay here as long as you want. My mother is fine with that."

"You are too nice. I don't know what to say or how to thank you."

Reb wasn't able to hold her tears anymore. She started crying heavily, all the things that had happened over the last few days contributing to her flood of tears. Mirza turned off the cream lamp and left the room. He didn't want Reb to be ashamed of her tears.

Reb was bouncing on the top of the clouds, but she was afraid of falling off.

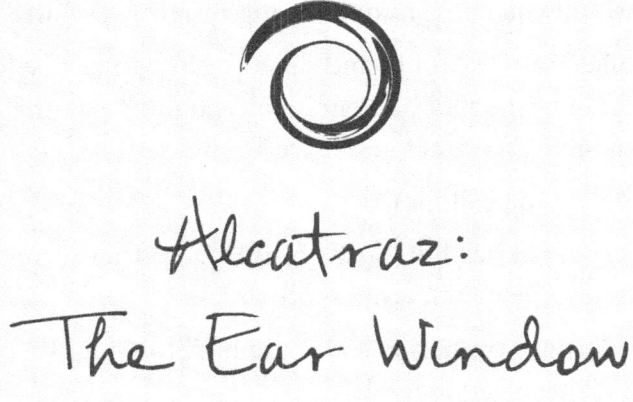

Alcatraz: The Ear Window

Nicole was not able to let the right noises in. There was a construction site nearby and all the machines were on. The lawnmower and the leaf collector were working in the garden. Moreover, there were sirens: ambulances and fire trucks. As if they were not enough, there was a party at the neighbor's house and the music was loud.

Nicole's shadow ran to the windows to close them. The noises coming through the ear window marched round the house. With every closed window, the noise army withdrew a little. Their boot prints were on the carpets. They were marching in the chaos.

Nicole was under attack from these noises. She couldn't live to a cinema sound system all the time. It was impossible to get used to the noises coming through her ear windows.

When she had closed all her windows, she became aware of the noises inside. A baby voice was inside Nicole; her inner child was crying. It was the millionth time that she had ignored herself, but her shadow was determined.

"I want to hear myself."

She became deaf to the dominant voice of her soul and heart. Listening to her inner voice was sometimes was like hearing the walking of an ant.

■

TWENTY-FIFTH SCENE

Meltem opened the door with *Let me realize myself* written on. Nicole was laying on Meltem's bed with her hands on her belly, smiling and looking at the ceiling.

Meltem put her bag on the table.

"Oh, my darling, make yourself comfortable. Get in my bed, sleep if you want. Girl, gather yourself together!"

She hit Nicole's knee. Nicole didn't bat an eyelid. Meltem got angry as she had to ask for permission to sit on her own bed.

"Tell me what happened. Come on!"

Nicole was playing with her red ringlets. She was dreamy.

"I'm talking to you! Come on, tell me what happened. Why did you come here in such a hurry, hey?"

"Okay, don't get too excited."

Nicole was trying to figure out how to tell her the news.

"I'm pregnant!"

Meltem opened her eyes wide and her mouth followed them. She slowly stood up from the bed and closed her mouth.

"What? By whom? Oh, Nik!"

"Tom. You know, we went to the room at the party. It happened that night. I can't believe it. Meltem, think about it, I'm going to be a mother. Argh! Should we lock the door? My voice won't be heard from downstairs, will it?"

Nicole tried to calm down, but she couldn't tune her voice. She was either yelling or whispering.

"I can't believe you, Nicole. That's why you wore the witch costume at the party—when you said, 'Whatever I do in this costume will be excused.' Your intention was to get out of your sin? You're only sixteen, how is it nice to have a baby at that age? How can you possibly raise a child without a father? You are not even married. I hope my mom does not hear about this or our friendship is over."

Meltem was strolling about her room as if she was the one going to have the baby. Nicole didn't care about anything she said till the last sentence.

"Well, it is my mom who should be hearing about this. I don't know what to do. My mom always puts condoms in the cookie jar in the kitchen. She keeps saying 'Don't get pregnant!' because she doesn't want to lose her babysitter. You know I always babysit Tamara, her daughter from that Japanese guy. I'll be my own baby's babysitter finally."

"You're still saying that you're going to be a mother? I'm going crazy! Hey, what happened to Betie, the friend with benefits?"

"She was temporary, you know."

"Then you are the permanent one? Nice!"

"Shut up, Melo! Can't you listen to me for a moment? Sit down here and calm down, please."

Meltem sat on the chair next to her study.

"I am listening now."

"You are very lucky, Meltem. You have a great mother. I think Nuray..."

TWENTY-FIFTH SCENE

"Nicole, please stop praising my mom. Take her, she can be your mom too."

Meltem threw a green pillow at her.

"No, you don't know anything. Listen, I have never felt like I am valued. I don't think Mom even likes me."

"No, that can't be true!" Meltem hadn't expected such an emotional speech and she wanted to make Nicole feel better by denying the truth.

"Please, don't interrupt me!" Nicole was determined to tell her everything. "You know, I have never met my father. My mother got pregnant outside of marriage, just like me. She might always have seen me as stealing her youth, I don't know. When she got pregnant with the Japanese guy's child, I did all of the housework. I even cooked. Then what happened? I became the babysitter. 'Why is it so bad to have to look after your sister?' you may ask. You are right, but when you both have the same mother and she treats her like a princess and you like a dog, it hurts. You may ask, 'Are you jealous of a little kid?' but my mom doesn't make it easier for me. Mom broke up with Tamara's father a long time ago, but he sends money every month for her and wants to be sure she is well cared for. That's why Mom is so careful around her, otherwise he will stop sending money. Every day after school, I take care of Tamara. When Mother comes home, she asks about Tamara without even looking at my face. She only cares about her because of the money, or maybe because she is so small."

Meltem thought about her little brother. She usually escaped having to play with him by saying she'd got homework. There were eleven years between them, but she couldn't remember a time when she'd had to look after him. Maybe if her mother worked like Nicole's mother did she would have to help out, but she didn't tell any of this to Nicole. Nicole telling her everything was slowly melting the ice in Meltem's heart. It was hard for Nicole to tell the naked truth, so she wasn't looking at Meltem's face. Instead she was hugging the green pillow Meltem had thrown at her.

"Okay, Nicole, but she is your mother."

"That's not the end of the story. She comes home every night drunk with a different man and I can't sleep because of the noises they make. Why do you think I listen to music so loud? I try to get lost in the music, but I haven't been successful yet. When I don't hear their voices, I don't feel that bad."

"Wait, was that why you were wearing ear plugs at the party?"

"I was scared of speaking that night. I was ashamed of what I had done. I felt like if I didn't hear my voice, I wouldn't feel bad about making that mistake. I thought everything that had happened would just have been a picture. I was drunk. And for the first time in my life Tom made me feel like I was special. Being special to someone is very important to me and that was my thanks to him. Do you understand me, Meltem?"

"I do, Nicole."

"Everybody says they get me, sometimes even my mom, but nobody actually does. You can say you see, but you can't say you've live my life."

"You're right, I don't get you. Have you told Tom?"

"No, not yet."

"So, am I the first person to hear it?"

"Yes, you are. Whether he wants it or not, I'll have the baby. This kid is my salvation, I'll be alive with this baby. This kid will be my home and my peace."

She covered her face with her hands to prevent tears from falling, but she was unsuccessful. Meltem hugged Nicole. She smelled apple shampoo from her curly hair and a sweet perfume. The beginning of motherhood smelled so innocent, like a baby cologne.

TWENTY-FIFTH SCENE

"I'm sorry" was the only thing that Meltem could say. Her mouth was dry again because of her tears.

Nuray knocked at the door and opened it without waiting for an answer.

"Girls, here is some cake for you."

When she saw the two girls hugging and crying, she was even more curious about what was going on, but she couldn't ask. The cake trick hadn't worked.

★

Sabahat called out to Nuray to hurry. Nuray got up from her bed and ran to her mother's room. She couldn't find her there and got even more worried.

"Where are you, Mom?"

"I'm here. Come!"

The voice was coming from the bathroom. Nuray opened the bathroom door.

"Mom, what happened?" She was trying hard not to laugh as the bathroom had become a small lake and the towels were swimming in it.

"I couldn't sleep so I decided to take a bath, then..."

"You wanted to clean the bathroom and used lots of water, but it didn't go anywhere so you panicked and used all the towels, right Mom?"

"Yes, but this bathroom doesn't have a drain. It's broken."

"No, it's not. The bathrooms here don't have drains like we have in Turkey."

"Then how do you wash the bathroom floor?"

"We don't, Mom."

"What's the world coming to?"

"We wipe the floor, like this."

Nuray took the towels from the floor.

"They don't call them 'dirty foreigners' for nothing, then."

"Don't say that, Mom!"

"Why shouldn't I? There is no bidet, no drain in the bathroom. They enter the house with shoes on—is it really clean that way?"

"They take a shower twice a day."

"If they took a dozen showers, I wouldn't call them clean."

"Whatever, Mom. Go to sleep, I'll finish here tomorrow. Nothing will happen. Good night!"

Sabahat felt ashamed like a scolded child. Her cheeks blushed and she left the room. Nuray was still laughing. She was glad her mother had come, but she wasn't sure she could stop the flood coming too.

TWENTY-SIXTH SCENE

Cihan didn't know how much deeper he would go while he was getting high. Getting high constantly was like diving without an oxygen tube. He felt like he was flying while he was skiing. He would be on the ground, going as fast as the steep mountain was high. He was here to get lost, to become white in this whiteness.

The snowstorm had started, but Cihan was still skiing despite all the warnings from the staff. He had been the only person on the lift going up to the ski slope one more time. If he hadn't bribed the person in charge, he wouldn't have been on the lift at all.

A rescue crew was waiting for Cihan at the bottom of the hill.

"Sir, that was very dangerous. We will have to cancel your membership. You can continue to stay at the hotel, but you are banned from skiing here."

"This is ridiculous!" Cihan was so angry he felt like he'd bust a blood vessel. "Edom, tell them I am okay."

"I can't. I warned you not to go up again."

"Okay, cancel my membership. I don't care, there are plenty of other ski centers."

"We are only doing our duty. We also fired the person on duty on the lift."

"Okay, do it then."

Cihan took off his shoes angrily. His face was red from the cold. Edom was slogging through the snow, following Cihan.

"Hey, Cihan, wait for me!"

"Why? You are the one told on me, traitor."

"What should I have done? I couldn't see you for half an hour because of the snowstorm. I thought you were dead, you damn retard!"

"Look, is this my dead body?"

"Not gonna happen again, I promise"

"Naturally it's not gonna happen again. There is no point in staying at this hotel. We'll leave tomorrow!"

Cihan and Edom unzipped their coats as soon as they were in the lobby. They were walking fast and didn't talk at all in the elevator. When they were in front of room 324, Edom opened the door with his white card. Cihan lay on the bed with his shoes on.

Edom sat at the table and tried to change the subject.

"You've got a message from Lara and your phone rang while you were skiing."

"From Lara? Strange!"

Hi, Cihan, can you send me the info about the ski center you went to? If it is nice, we want to go with some friends.

Cihan called Lara. Edom listened to the conversation as Cihan went onto the balcony and gave her the information about the place. As if he had not just been talking about leaving, he was now recommending the place.

Cihan came inside, played with the curtains then went onto the balcony again. He couldn't stand still for excitement while talking on the phone to Lara. His face was glowing and he was moving from one place to another.

TWENTY-SIXTH SCENE

Edom was aware of his excitement and this made him angry. He took a beer from the mini bar then closed its door.

"We are here for a couple of days more if you'd like to come..."

Edom's mind blew. He went to the door of the balcony and cursed Cihan quietly.

"Hmmm, you are thinking about coming next month? Okay, we'll talk again when I get back."

Edom spread his legs on the chair. He was wearing his gray shorts and his black athletics shirt. He was holding his beer with two hands and waiting for an explanation from Cihan

"What do you think you are doing? You chew me up then you are a sweetheart to someone else."

"Lara is a good girl."

"How do you know? And am I bad?" Edom threw the bottle on the ground.

"No, you are no such thing. You just speak politely with women."

"Is that all? There is nothing else between you two?

Suddenly Cihan lost his temper.

"That is none of your business. Are you my mom or dad? There is nothing between us, and even if there was, it wouldn't be any of your business. You are talking as if she could be your rival."

"None of my business, is it?"

Edom slammed the door and went out wearing nothing but shorts and an athletics shirt. He escaped from the fire inside him and went into the cold.

It was the first time that Cihan had seen Edom that angry; moreover, it was the first time Edom had called him to account. He didn't know what to do, but he was sure he didn't want to follow Edom. Instead he watched from the window. Cihan saw how people in winter clothes were looking at Edom; they must have been thinking he was crazy. When they began pointing at him, Cihan couldn't stand there any longer. Taking Edom's coat, Cihan went out.

"Don't touch me!"

Cihan grabbed Edom by the neck and threw him on the ground, filling his mouth with a handful of snow. Edom responded in kind and a snowball fight began. Yet their real fight wouldn't be so much fun.

Alcatraz: The Knife

Julie touched the knife lying in the cupboard, and then touched her heart.

Words spilled from her tongue like blood. She was talking to the knife.

"Knife, divide an apple or a pear or a loaf of bread, but don't divide my soul. I want to live as a whole, I'm happy that way. I have also been unhappy, but I don't mind it. Just don't touch me with your sharp side. Don't cut me. I want to live as I want. I know if my soul is cut, it will hurt. Don't let it hurt. My hands are shaking holding you. Don't cut me, knife.

"I had a paper cut recently which turned my eyes red. I had a love cut which made me drink blood. If you have to cut me, cut my fake side, my jealous side, my proud side or my sour side.

"I'm sad with all my innocence and smiling eyes. I'm sad at my history of sadness. Now cut these words and these pages. Feel pity for your soul!"

TWENTY-SEVENTH SCENE

She was working as a cashier in one of the big supermarkets. On Thursday February 21 she worked half a day then went home and hung her brown jacket on the back of the door. It was dark all around. She saw the empty bottles on the floor; Mark must be at home.

There was some mumbling in the small room. She went slowly to the cabin in the corner of the garage. She heard panting noises from inside and words she couldn't understand.

"Johnson must be at school, so what is Mark doing in there? Is he cheating on me?"

Mark put Johnson in the penalty room whenever he got angry with him. Julie let him do that as she wasn't able to handle Mark. He had been unemployed for months, spending his days fixing something in the garage.

The door of the cabin was closed; there was only a bar of light. She didn't know what to do. Was she supposed to open the door without knocking or knock on it first? She realized there was a little hole in it and decided to check from there.

Johnson was sitting on Mark's lap wearing only his basketball T-shirt. He had a bitter look on his face as if he was in pain. Mark was holding Johnson's penis with one hand and his neck with the other.

TWENTY-SEVENTH SCENE

Julie felt short of breath. She closed her mouth and ran to the kitchen, going up and down, trying to figure out what to do. She took a knife in her hand a couple of times, but then put it on the table again. She had to let Mark know she was home. She opened the garage door and Mark immediately left the cabin and checked his surroundings. Seeing nothing, he entered the kitchen.

Mark was a huge man, but Julie's pain was bigger. She held the knife and aimed it at him.

"I saw you, you damn cunt!"

Her eyes were mad.

"Stop, hey, calm down. What have you seen, you crazy woman?"

Julie got even madder at his laid back attitude. She pointed at his open zipper.

"I have seen this, you filth. Tell me what you were doing to my son."

"Stop, bitch!"

Mark made her drop the knife while pressing her to the wall. He bit her neck. She had no power to fight back and sat desperately on the ground.

*

"This is it, Reb. I left home that day while the garage door was open. I wasn't able to handle it when Mom found out. I returned home a week later, but something even worse happened. I can't tell you now, though."

He was ashamed of his truth. Explaining his story to someone had made him feel like he was in the spotlight.

TWENTY-EIGHTH SCENE

"I don't want a baby. Good luck to you, Nicole!"

Tom raised his hand and bowed to the audience, smiling. The audience was his classmates. Nicole got mad at them.

"Why are you staring at me? Is it really so interesting? Ordinary things happen."

Nicole was surprised at herself.

"Ordinary things happen? I'm talking nonsense. It's not like every day I get pregnant or everyone becomes a mother at such an early age. I meant this could happen to anyone. Whatever, I've got bigger problems, like my mother."

Meltem watched Nicole from a distance, and then followed her to the door. Nicole looked like she was wearing a red hat because she had tied her curly hair on top of her head. She was wearing pink earrings and had attached her green horn-rimmed glasses to her black and white striped shirt. She had put on more makeup than usual, but she couldn't hide her pain. She was trying to hide her real face from herself.

*

"He said get an abortion! Stupid boy. He said he was too young to be a father and it was my problem. I hope he rots in hell!"

TWENTY-EIGHTH SCENE

"Okay, Nicole, calm down. You already knew Tom wouldn't want the baby. Why are you upset?"

"Yes, but I thought for a moment that he would help me. Now that possibility has faded away. Oh!"

Nicole covered her face.

"I have a headache. I'm going home."

"Wait a minute. Is this headache caused by the drugs you use?"

"I guess so. Sometimes I think I'm going mad, Nicole."

"I think you should stop taking them, immediately."

"It's not that easy. I have been using them for five months, I'm an addict now. I can't stand giving up."

"Carrying on is gonna be more dangerous. Stop immediately!"

"It's easy for you to say, Nicole. If you know so much, find a solution to the problem in your belly."

Meltem started going on her way, but then stopped and asked: "What about your mother? Isn't she the real problem?"

"Yes. I've told Tom, now it's time to tell Mom."

"How are you going to do that?"

"I have a perfect plan. Hope it works!"

Treasure Island: Bridge

Cihan said nothing to Edom and left him on the hill. He was going to the Golden Gate Bridge without knowing the reason why. The only thing he knew was crossing the bridge would make him feel better.

You could fall through the gaps in a broken bridge, and some bridges were underwater. The bridges strong enough to endure the wind would be long-lasting, while the ones on the river had to be even stronger to endure the tide.

The bridges had to be wind and earthquake-proof no matter what they were made off. They were everywhere: in the middle of a city or in a garden far away. Humans made the bridges and demolished them; they either connected people or the opposite happened.

This world was a bridge between two other worlds.

One could make a connection every day: between history and the future; today and tomorrow; before and after. The gaps were filled with these connections.

The bridges that connected the soul and the truth were only built with faith. You could only cross without falling if you believed in Him. There was a huge gap between the soul and the truth; it was only possible to cross this gap with Him.

TWENTY-NINTH SCENE

"Hey, Cihan, come here! The view is superb. Look, I love this angle most."

Edom framed the view with his fingers.

"Golden Gate is stunning, like a woman with long red hair. Don't you think so? Let me take a photo of you near this tree!"

Edom focused the lens of the camera and waved at Cihan.

"Come on!"

"I don't want a photo. Say what you are going to say, I need to go and write a paper."

Edom lowered the camera, subdued. He sat cross-legged on the ground, avoiding eye contact with Cihan. Cihan sat beside him. He didn't know what Edom was going to say, but he felt uneasy. Edom had invited him to Golden Gate and implied it was something important. They had been in a good place since the holiday at Lake Tahoe so he didn't want any trouble now.

Edom looked at Cihan strangely. He didn't say anything but touched his lips.

Cihan pushed Edom.

"What did you say?"

He threw a punch at Edom's stomach. Edom was motionless and only made a small sound. Cihan punched him constantly till Edom bent down.

"It's nothing new, I have been this way for a long time."

"Shut up!"

There was nowhere to place himself on that hill. Cihan was on the ground, but actually felt like he was down in the earth. He felt like he didn't know the city he had been living in for years. He wasn't talking in a language he had used for years. He didn't feel the pain he had felt at first. He had lost all his senses. He didn't know anyone who felt so much for him and was so close to him. He wasn't sure of himself, or the guy he had known for years. His dear friend was crying for him. It was a very complex puzzle.

"It can't be happening," one side of him was saying, while the other said, "Why not?" He wished there had been someone on the bridge to prevent him from losing his mind. He wanted to burn what he had heard then throw it to the wind. He saw Edom in the clouds; he heard Edom's voice in the wind.

He was walking on the cycle lane on Golden Gate. He wanted to do something different and became different. He wanted to cross the bridge inside him.

He had left Edom five minutes ago. There was no turning back now he had learned the information he wished he never had. Why did Edom decide to tell him? That made him feel sick as he knew he had potential to say "Why not?" Even though he said he had no intention, his love for Edom was powerful. He was sure the same was true for Edom, but some loves should be kept secret forever.

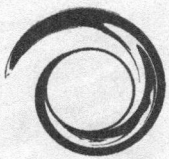

Alcatraz: Telephone

There were different melodies ringing inside Nuray. Not one single part of her answered them. There were calls every day at the same time, but her inner ears didn't hear them. They ignored the melodies not to prevent her happiness, but to remain emotionless.

Life was tiring for Nuray. When she didn't hear the melodies, it was easy to ignore the exhaustion. She wasn't able to cope with her life outside, so how could she handle her inner life? Nobody knew about the storms on her shores.

One day Nuray's consciousness made her answer one of the calls. She was waiting beside the telephone when the dead phone came to life. She tried to press the button to answer, but it didn't work. She tried harder, but still it didn't work. This was no hide and seek game anymore as she knew someone had called her. It was she who had decided not be reached, but she now lost something from her name.

N

U

R

A

Y.

THIRTIETH SCENE

Nuray was cleaning the kitchen in her orange tracksuit and black velvet headband. After sending the kids to school, she had gone outside to take out the garbage. The gardener had mowed the grass so there was a fresh grass smell all around. She smiled at the sun.

Her neighbor caught her eye as she was looking around. She was hugging a man, but Nuray was sure he wasn't her husband, Robert. Robert was mid-height and African American, but the guy Michele was kissing was big, bald and white. Michele got into his car, and Nuray froze with the garbage in her hand.

"They have two kids—shame. Poor Robert."

Then she thought about herself. She knew her husband was cheating on her with Linda, yet she continued to live and sleep with him. She pitied herself. Her mother was there to support her, but she never mentioned anything about it. Everybody made a deal and played a game in which everyone seemed happy.

Nuray went to shop for groceries. On the way to the supermarket, her phone rang. It was her neighbor, Michele. Nuray felt curiosity pique. What was Michele going to say? Had she seen Nuray in the garden watching her?

Nuray put the phone on silent when she stopped at the red lights. She panicked as if she was the one cheating on her husband. Her phone was still ringing on the seat. She waited for a pot-bellied

THIRTIETH SCENE

man in a white shirt and a tall woman to cross the road with their coffees in hand. Were Linda and Şahin like that?

She heard the message alert and listened to it immediately.

"Hello, dear Nuray, it's Michele. I'm gonna ask something from you. I will be very busy today. Could you pick up my kids from school at three? You will need to reply quickly so I can call the school to let them know."

Nuray took a deep breath, relieved Michele hadn't seen her. Then she realized Michele was the guilty one, not Nuray. However, she had promised Michele that she would pick up her kids whenever needed. She had no excuses, but she didn't want to be a part of that sin. How she could possibly do Michele's chores while Michele was having an affair with that guy? She didn't say no, though, as she didn't have many friends. Michele was one of them.

Nuray entered the supermarket, but she had forgotten to take the list she had made beforehand. She was walking up and down the aisles, thinking about Michele's affair and the twins. Michele's husband, Robert, was a mail man while Michele worked in a bank, so she earned more money than him. Nuray wondered whether the one who earned more had a right to cheat.

She put a lot of things into her trolley but forgot to get the things she needed.

She examined the personal care products for a long time. She read the label of a new shampoo which promised wonderful things and bought one, blaming her old shampoo for her curly and weak hair. Her favorite part of the supermarket was the cosmetics section. Şahin made fun of her as she didn't like wearing makeup at all, but she always ended up buying a lipstick. Today, she decided to buy a purple one as she was a little jealous of Michele.

She had another reason for buying it, though.

She left the bags in the kitchen and lay on the velvet sofa in the living room. There was no sound around; her mother must have been sleeping. She realized there was a spider on the window. Since moving to San Francisco, she'd had problems with the spiders. She saw them everywhere, but got used to them after a while. She only screamed when she saw one in the kitchen. All her children laughed at her because of that. She went to the window, moved the curtains and saw the spider's web. She didn't want to clean it away as she thought she had no right to demolish a creature's home.

Alcatraz: Riot

What she had pressed inside her was now overflowing to the outside. What she saw, knew and gathered from life didn't fit into this prison. The ideas were rioting, they had no patience. They wanted to be free again. Their escape worked against Lara, but also for her.

There were lots of ideas flowing through her cells. There was no guardian around to hold them. The riot in Alcatraz had just started. It was bloody, yet it was natural to kill and be killed. There was no return journey till her foreignness ended and she began to feel local.

THIRTY-FIRST SCENE

Lara was passing through the Japanese Tea Garden. The color of the flowers gave her a new sense. Beauty was to be aware of your own culture in another culture's garden. The purpose of her visit was to drink some green tea and smell the bergamot and taste the jasmine.

Passing through the small temples, she had to squint due to the flashes of the cameras. She watched the fish in the water from the small wooden bridges. The roads were going up; bridges in all cultures are about to going up. The differences build new gardens in our minds. We put other colors and smells to what we had already have. Gardens make us regard our cities from a higher place, adding soils and putting new ideas in our own homes .

Lara was watching a Japanese show in America. The taste of their tea was completely different than the tea she had been drinking for years. The difference was nice. It was worth going to the other side of the world and exploring herself. Not only her viewpoint but her whole being changed with the tea she was drinking.

It was almost lunchtime when she began walking the streets of China Town. She took off her blue cardigan and tied it around her waist The California sun was quick to warm everything it touched. On the other hand, its wind was peevish. She wasn't able to stand against it without a jacket.

THIRTY-FIRST SCENE

This city was like a human being, having different aspects. These aspects showed themselves in different ways through different cultures. One city represented many other cities. Every eye looking at it saw it differently.

Lara loved walking around the city, but this time it was enough. She was so tired she left and returned to the sofa.

★

Sadaf entered Lara's room with two cups of coffee.

"I'm wasted, Sadaf. Both Japan and China were too much in one day. Look at my eyes!"

She made her eyes slant.

"Hahaha, Lara! Try as you like, you can't make yourself look Asian without making those huge eyes smaller. I know the Japanese garden is nice, but what's up with China Town?"

Lara answered without thinking: "Myself! Do you know, I'm an alien in this city, and so is China Town. But we are both world citizens."

"Feeling like a stranger makes you feel better? How?"

"Yes, I don't feel so alone!"

"Right, but there are lots of foreign people living in this city. Look at me, I'm originally Pakistani."

She sucked her lips into her mouth. She always did this; it was a nervous twitch. Once Lara had thought she did this because she was ashamed of what she had said and thought she probably shouldn't keep speaking.

Lara pulled Sadaf's ponytail.

"That's why I'm staying with you, to feel my difference more."

Sadaf was used to Lara's jokes, but still she screamed.

"Oh, don't!" Sadaf sat beside Lara and prepared to ask her something. "Why do you feel better by being different, foreign and—what did you call it? —a loner?"

"It doesn't make me feel better, Sadaf, but it makes me more me. Think about it: I came here from overseas. I'm far away from my country, yet close to me. You can't see what's very close to your eyes, right?"

Sadaf tried to look as though she understood.

"Can you see a beautiful painting when you put your face against it? It's like that. Getting away from myself made me closer to me. Never mind, I'm feeling deep and talking nonsense."

Sadaf felt sorry for Lara, then realized she was late. While Lara was putting the dishes from the night before into the dishwasher, Sadaf prepared to leave the house.

"Don't be sad, Lara, I'll pray for you!"

"Thanks," Lara said and came to the door with the towel in her hand. "Take care"

Lara closed the door. She realized that she hadn't prayed for a long time, or maybe the time felt longer because she didn't pray. She had lots of reasons to pray, but she had just given up. She needed to go and apologize by praying.

She put on some music, needing an outside sound or she would have had to listen to her conscience. It was talking to her, but she decided to turn a deaf ear.

THIRTY-SECOND SCENE

Meltem read the note and shook her head, looking at Nicole. At the end of the class she found her friend near the basketball court.

"Hey, what's up?"

"Meltem, they called me, I'm so scared!"

Nicole suddenly began hyperventilating.

"Who called you? Why are you scared?"

"They called me from *Teen Show*, the one 'bout teen mothers. I told you I'd written an email to them? It was three weeks ago, so I thought they wouldn't call."

"Okay, isn't this what you wanted?"

"I don't know, Meltem. Do you think it is a good idea? Mom will kill me if she sees me on TV!"

"She won't. It's for the best. Would you prefer her to find out when your belly gets bigger? When is the show?"

"Tomorrow night!"

"Whaaat?"

"You're scared now too, aren't you."

"I am excited. I didn't know it would be that soon. You told me you had no other choice"

"That's right, I don't!"

Nicole was chewing the nail polish from her fingers again.

"Okay, darling. Everything will be fine, don't you worry."

*

There were a lot of lamps around the mirror. Her fingernails were purple because of her excitement; her index finger was bleeding as she bit it. She took a napkin and pressed it on her finger. Nobody could see it, but all of her was bleeding.

The hairdresser fixed some combs in her hair then a short childish woman came over. She had very short hair, a snake tattoo and no breasts. After saying hi, she put a lot of powder on Nicole's face. Even her eyebrows were lost under the powder. Without changing her expression, the woman continued to make her up. Nicole had never hated makeup more in her whole life as she knew she was preparing for a facedown. She would confess her sin then try to hold onto the love of the woman who had given birth to her.

"I have a baby inside, Mom, just like you had me inside you."

She repeated the words she was going to say. The audience was oblivious, but Nicole had already lived the show a million times in her head.

The makeup room was getting crowded. A woman with a radio yelled: "Last five minutes!"

Nicole needed to pee urgently. She only went half an hour ago, but it was impossible for her to continue like that.

"You are ready, young lady," said the small woman. Nicole tried to ask her questions to calm herself down, but the woman didn't answer any of them. Nicole became even more nervous because of that.

THIRTY-SECOND SCENE

"Where is the toilet?" asked Nicole to the program assistant with long blond hair.

"I'll take you there, but hurry please. We have only four minutes. Don't forget to answer every question, don't give long answers. Please don't cry!"

Nicole looked older than her years in her mustard dress with lace arms. She rushed to the toilet in her high heels, closed the door and waited to pee, but not a single drop came out. She always had trouble peeing when she was stressed. Heeding the blond woman's warning, she gave up and washed her hands. She looked at the mirror for the last time and said, "I'm ready", even though she was sure she wasn't. She would never be ready, but she had no choice. It would happen now or never. She had chosen now because she was afraid of never.

The opening credits had started. The screams were coming from the studio full of people. The assistant kept giving directives to her.

"Walk from the right then sit on the chair. Talk looking at the camera with the light on. Sit up straight and don't move a lot."

"*And Nicole!*" said the show's presenter.

Nicole entered the studio. There was no going back now. Even if it meant she would have no place to go back to that night, she was about to tell the truth in front of the TV cameras.

"Hi, Nicole. Welcome! Please sit down."

The applause and music stopped. Nicole was a little bit overweight and wearing a miniskirt, so she had to sit accordingly. Surprisingly, she sat up straight, smiling.

"Nicole, we have heard your story and watched your video. Now it's your turn to talk. Are you ready to talk with your mother?"

"Yes," answered Nicole without thinking.

There was loud applause in the studio. People were screaming her name when the tension music started. There was also the sound of a telephone, dialing her mother.

Diiiiitt diiiiit diiiiitt!

Nicole decided there were two less things for her to do now: putting on makeup and calling her mother.

"Hi, Rose, we are calling you from *Teen Show*. You're on the air. How are you?"

"I'm well, but I don't understand why you've called me. Is it a wrong number?"

"No, madam. Your daughter Nicole is with us and she wants to tell you something. Will you please listen to her?"

"Hmmm…okay, I'm listening."

All the eyes, cameras and lights were on Nicole.

"Mom, I'm pregnant!"

She confessed in one breath as if she had stayed underwater too long and needed to breathe as soon as she surfaced.

There were thunders of applause in the studio, but Nicole couldn't understand what they were celebrating—her being pregnant at a young age or having the courage to confess it on the TV.

Rose was speechless. There was only the sound of her breathing. Nicole began crying.

"Hey, Rose, are you there?" the presenter asked.

"Yes, I am."

"Do you want to talk with your daughter?"

"Yes. Nicole, who is the father?"

"Tom."

"And I have told you not to have sex without protection. You know the cookie jar in the kitchen?"

THIRTY-SECOND SCENE

"Wait a minute, what is this cookie jar?"

"Well, my mom puts condoms in the cookie jar in the kitchen."

"An interesting method."

"I'm sorry, Mom!" Nicole was playing with the napkin in her hand.

"Are you sorry? That doesn't alter the fact you are having a baby."

Nicole was now crying on the shoulder of the presenter. Some people in the audience were also crying, their mascara running. Nicole realized why the short woman hadn't put mascara on her eyes: she must have known everybody here would cry and the audience wouldn't like looking at black eyes.

"Won't you help her, Rose? She is very sad and she's your daughter."

"No, never. Good luck, Nicole! Find yourself a place to stay!"

Rose hung up. Nicole knew what was coming; she felt a déjà vu. The assistant came in the commercial break and helped her to leave the studio. She was so gentle as if she was treating an old lady, and Nicole was feeling old at that moment.

An African-American girl was on next. Nicole wanted to warn her not to go on, but decided not to. Maybe her mom would forgive her.

"Mom, didn't you get pregnant at a young age? I don't even know my father. You went through the same things as me and you told me your story. Our destiny is the same, Mom, so why do you condemn me? Or is this your own punishment?"

Nicole was only able to say these words in her mind. She was a homeless mother now, a homeless home for her baby.

THIRTY-THIRD SCENE

When Cihan returned home it was very late at night and there was no one around. While he was opening the door slowly he must have made some noise as his mother came down. Cihan left the keys on the countertop and said his regular words.

"Mom, why aren't you sleeping again?"

"Why do you have to ask, Cihan? Your phone was off. I thought something had happened to you."

"Nothing happened, my battery died. I was with Edi."

"Okay, are you hungry?" She opened the fridge door. "We have…"

"Mom, I'm not hungry at all. All I want is sleep, I'm so tired."

His posture was screaming "Leave me alone" so Nuray sensed something was wrong with him. She knew he wouldn't answer her questions so she needed another way to find out what it was. Cihan was determined not to give anything away, so Nuray gave up and they both went upstairs.

Cihan lay down on his bed without putting on his pajamas. The home was warm, his sweater was too much. Actually everything was too much for him. It would be so nice never to have heard what he had heard that day. He began thinking about the bridge, leaving Edom on it, losing his childhood friend. He was mostly sad about the reason for losing him.

THIRTY-THIRD SCENE

Every scene hurt him. Even though he didn't want to think about it, the scenes kept running before his eyes. He was trying to escape from them, which made him more tired than running miles. He had participated in the San Francisco marathon for the last five years, but he had never felt this tired afterwards. Tiredness of the body was nothing compared to tiredness of the mind and soul. The body would heal itself in a few days, but the mind and soul would be tired forever.

The fire inside him was getting bigger. He put his head under his pillow, yet nothing would help as his soul was overflowing from his body.

He opened the windows besides his bed. The moon was a thin slice of apple in the sky. He waited for daylight in the darkest of the night.

*

Cihan,

I already regret what I told you. When I saw you running on the bridge, very bad things came into my mind so I watched you till you left. I never wanted to hurt you. You've been my best friend for years. Now I have other feelings for you that I can't help feeling, but let's pretend I don't. Please forget what I told you. I know this will be hard and you will think about it whenever you see me, but don't let our friendship be over. Let's climb the mountains, run the marathon, drink coffee together, ski in Tahoe and share everything. Remember when we were kids we used to lie on the grass and watch the sky? Every cloud resembled a different thing. Can we be that innocent again?

E.

Cihan checked his mailbox again in the morning, but this time he deleted Edom's email without reading it. As soon as he had deleted it he regretted it as he wondered what Edom had written. Was it a joke? It couldn't be as Edom had cried in front of him. Cihan had never seen Edom crying before.

Cihan stood up and walked past his caricature on the wall, moved the ocean encyclopedia. He took the vase and sugar bowl and put them on the top shelf. There was a picture on the corner by the clock made from crown caps of two young men hugging each other in front of a yellow car. Cihan took the photo and put it face down. He finally took the locked black box. Edom and Cihan had gathered some stones from the shore of Los Angeles and put them in that box. He kicked the surfboard Edom had given him as a present. The surfboard fell down and Cihan climbed on it, moving from his home to the waves of Santa Cruz. The waves were slapping his face and Cihan gulped lots of water.

The waves were different. They became the person and Cihan was the wave. A storm was coming from his mouth, making white surf.

*

The only thing Edom had learned from his father, Rannan Mendel, that he held onto passionately was surfing. Cihan had never gone surfing with Edom, despite his persistence, till he lost a bet. The two young men then went to Santa Cruz on a Sunday morning.

Edom told Cihan that he would teach him to surf, but Edom glided on the waves and left him on the board. Edom looked like he was ice-skating while Cihan was stepping on the wave's feet, trying to dance.

Cihan was troubled by these memories.

THIRTY-FOURTH SCENE

Linda hurried onto a plane from Las Vegas to San Francisco. Şahin had called Linda a lot, but she didn't answer the calls. Their boss had been surprised to get a letter of resignation as their projects were going well. Linda left the company she had worked with for eight years, pregnant and in a lot of pain. She left her dream guy and Turkish food, liking mustaches, drinking lots of tea, taking off her shoes and her desire to visit Istanbul.

Linda rushed to the hospital the day she arrived. Now she was waiting to resign from having a baby inside her. She was going to resign from everything and have a clean start. Waiting was getting unbearable as there were baby noises all around. She thought about the baby who would have been able to scream if she had let him. She was resigning from motherhood even before she'd tried it.

An Indian doctor in a white coat entered the room and asked, "Are you ready?"

*

Linda was trying to walk with a nurse helping her. A door opened and she could see a mother breastfeeding a baby. He was swimming in a pure white stream; a stream linking baby and mother to each other. Linda fell down to her knees and began screaming. She had no more power.

Months ago she had decided to keep her baby and become a mother, but life and death were so closely connected that she had lost her baby in the delivery room.

*

Meltem and new mother Nicole looked at the woman screaming on the ground.

"I'll close the door so the baby will be more comfortable."

The door to motherhood was closed for Linda while the same door opened for Nicole.

*

Milk, warm, plain and sweet, streaming like a river in the throat, calm and sedate in the veins.

Humans meet milk when they first come into the world.

First the milk was white, then it turned dark.

*

Cihan was separating the vegetables on his plate. He wanted to be able to separate the sides of himself he didn't like too. What if he only felt the feelings he liked? His mother had made a vegetable dish and Cihan was only eating the meat in it. Nuray was angry at her son because of that, but she said nothing. She knew he was troubled.

Şahin was on his phone again. Every night he asked "How was your day?" then continued to check his emails or play games. Meltem was eating in a sleepy way. Her mother had woken her up to eat. She had to eat to grow up.

"How is the baby?"

THIRTY-FOURTH SCENE

"He is so sweet, Mom. You should see his tiny feet."

Şahin left his phone on the table.

"Which baby?"

"Nicole's," answered both Nuray and Meltem. Nuray explained more after taking a sip from her orange juice.

"Meltem's friend Nicole's baby."

Şahin didn't want to hear about any baby after his nightmare. He had never been able to contact Linda again. He was curious whether she'd had an abortion or not.

"Here your *Mevlana borek*, it's hot!"

"Oh, Mother! Please never leave us!" said Şahin.

"It seems I can't. Came here for six months and it has already been nine months." Sabahat answered her son-in-law while putting the *boreks* on plates.

"Mom, do you know what happened at the hospital? There was a beautiful blond woman standing in front of our open door and looking at us. Then she screamed and collapsed on the ground. The nurses rushed to help her but she could hardly walk. She must have lost her baby."

Şahin suddenly asked, "What did the woman look like?"

Nuray said, "How would you know?" She felt like she had heard this sentence before. Then, she decided she didn't believe what she had said. Nuray felt a moment of madness when she was at the table. There was no longer meaning to the actions they were performing at that time She would close her eyes when she didn't want to believe in something, as if losing her ability to see amounted to the same thing.

Sabahat realized something was wrong. She panicked like a mother whose child was crying on the feeding chair.

"Nuray, should we put out the candles on the table and move the lampshade here? Here all homes are dim. Not just yours, I look on the street and everybody's home is in darkness. Are you doing it to save electricity? Yet I can't see your faces."

"Okay, Mom," said Nuray laughing. Sabahat was happy that she had been able to distract her daughter.

THIRTY-FIFTH SCENE

As soon as Lara put the last dot in her project, her laptop froze. She hadn't saved the file so she panicked. She tried a few things, but they only caused her laptop to die completely. She had been writing for hours—was it really gone? Looking blankly at the screen in San Francisco Public Library, she took a sip from her jasmine green tea but spilled some on herself. She looked at her notes again, but she was tired and had no power to continue.

A hand touched her shoulder. She turned round and saw an African-American man in a yellow hood. He was the occupant of the street home she had stayed in. He smiled at her.

"Hey, what are you doing here?" She spoke loudly and only realized her mistake when people looked at her. "It's Joe, isn't it?"

"No, Joe is my dog. I'm Johnson."

"Of course, Johnson."

"I spend time here reading books or newspapers on the Internet. And, you know, the library is warmer than the street."

Lara looked around for a chair for Johnson, then said, "Let's go and get a coffee. I want to buy you a coffee to say thank you. What do you think?"

Johnson nodded and headed to the stairs. Lara couldn't put her things in her bag quickly enough. Johnson had already left, so she followed him running. It was a good opportunity for her project.

When she was on the stairs, she realized she had forgotten her jacket so she called out to Johnson, "Wait a little, please."

Johnson had already left the building. Lara got her jacket but had lost him. She opened the door. There was an old lady in a wheelchair entering the building so she waited for her to pass. The wind welcomed her when she finally went outside. She was familiar with San Francisco wind, which sent the sun with it so nobody knew whether it was warm or cold.

She saw Johnson with his dog Joe and approached them, trying hard not to make any sound.

"I thought you'd gone."

"I'm here."

"Well, I invited you for a coffee." She pointed at the coffee shop without taking her hands out of her pockets.

"Let's go," he said, pulling Joe's leash. Joe was a black-gray Keeshond. Johnson and Joe were walking ahead of Lara. She had to move quicker to catch them up.

He doesn't even know how to walk with someone. How strange, said Lara in her mind.

When the door opened, the bell rang. A young woman welcomed them into the coffee shop.

"You sit down in the corner, I'll get the coffees."

The café was hot. She was surprised as she thought every indoor place in America was cold. Most places kept the temperature down inside.

"I have been trying to call you to ask what you want, but you weren't looking at me!" Lara came to the table with two coffees in her hand and spoke as if she had known Johnson for years or was flirting with her boyfriend. When she realized, she apologized immediately.

THIRTY-FIFTH SCENE

"Well, I got mocha for us. Do you like it?"

"I do."

The time flew without them realizing. Lara was laughing, Johnson was laughing, and Lara was teasing him. When she looked at the clock, she couldn't believe it had been two hours.

Johnson saw her looking at the clock. "Shall we leave?" He didn't care about time as there was no time on the streets, but he took his coffee cup and threw it into the garbage then left the café. Lara didn't even have time to put on her jacket. He left without saying goodbye. Everything was over.

Lara got on the bus. Sadaf was calling.

"Where are you? Nuray, Meltem and Emir came to visit you but left after an hour. Why didn't you answer your phone?"

"Really? I had no idea, I was at the library."

"Of course, I'm sure. Do you know what time it is?"

"Okay, I went to the café with a friend afterwards. Sadaf, cut it out. I'm coming home now."

Tomorrow was the deadline for her project but it was still not ready. *That's because of Johnson,* she thought. The streets and homelessness were the ones to blame; Lara was innocent.

THIRTY-SIXTH SCENE

His eyes were open yet closed to the world. Sleeping with open eyes made him stop witnessing. He kept turning over and clawing the sheets. His neck was hurting on the pillow, but he didn't have any power to move to adjust it.

Cihan gave the sling he had been holding to Edom so the stone entered his own eye. He was somewhere unfamiliar between accepting and giving up.

Edom had told him if he hadn't been holding his hands they wouldn't have come to the place they now were. Cihan denied holding his hand, and it was this denial that hurt most. It had been five months since Cihan had left Edom and there had been no morning for Cihan since then.

THIRTY-SEVENTH SCENE

Kate had hidden her pregnancy from Rannan for five months. When he'd finally found out he had told her he wanted the kid but they would never marry. Kate didn't object.

Living in the same home was a lot harder with the baby. Living together without marriage was like playing house. Even though nobody knew, Kate felt like the house wasn't real.

Kate left her job at the bank right after the birth. When Edom was four years old, she homeschooled him. He learned everything in that home. There was no going to school; the school came to him. His mother was his teacher.

Rannan's interest in Kate went completely after Edom's birth. They lived in the same house as friends without sharing a bed or sex life. Kate felt angry with Edom as a result. Rannan would still have been in love with her if it hadn't have been for Edom.

Rannan was a busy man. When he was at home he taught Edom passages from the Torah and how to speak in Hebrew. When Edom began university, Kate had some health issues. She had to spend time at home so she chose to redecorate the house. Rannan Mandel was not ungenerous, so Kate spent as much money as she wanted, but she was not permitted to go out a lot so she was unhappy.

She seemed to have a home, but it was no different than a prison for her. Rannan's family had no respect for her. They thought a Christian woman had deceived their son and got pregnant. They didn't meet very often except for the holy days of Judaism. Edom's grandparents took Edom every two weeks to their fortress in Sausalito; Kate was never welcomed there so she regarded it as a fortress. She felt it was an injustice to blame everything on her; she was the mother of their grandson after all, but she had no power to go against the two old people. Whenever she complained about them to Rannan, he would answer, "I never promised you a rose garden."

Edom grew up in silent pain. That pain became a huge burden on his shoulders. His mother's emptiness affected him and he tried to fill that emptiness with Cihan.

*

Kate and Nuray had met in a shopping mall. Cihan had been eleven, while Edom was twelve. Rannan had never given permission for play days at their home so they had play days at Nuray's home. They met every two weeks, talking about their loneliness. Nuray complained about Şahin and Kate did the same thing with Rannan.

One day Kate told her secret to Nuray. Kate was crying while telling her story:

"We have been together for fifteen years and we're still not married. At first I didn't care about it as I am not a strict Christian and it was no problem for my family either. They didn't mind that I'd had a baby outside of marriage. Yet I'm understanding as I get older that marriage is a strong tie. It feels like I am holding onto the wing of an airplane. It was exciting at first, but now I have Edom and we are still not allowed in that plane. I don't know how much longer we can fly like that, but Rannan will never marry me as I am not Jewish."

She wiped her small red nose on her napkin and continued.

THIRTY-SEVENTH SCENE

"We can't be a family. Where is my home, Nuray? That white mansion looks black to me. I enter into that coffin every day. I would leave Rannan immediately if it wasn't for Edom. He is holding me back. It's not acceptable to do this to any woman, but Rannan's doing it to me, a nice and beautiful woman."

"What he will do to you?" Nuray still had difficulty speaking in English so she avoided it around the kids. Kate understood what Nuray was trying to say but didn't want to answer her. Nuray gave her a fresh napkin. She blew her nose loudly. Nuray still wasn't used to the loud blowing and laughing sounds of American people.

She didn't understand how a woman who never had to go on a diet or do housework would be that pessimist. Nobody's life was perfect, even though some seemed so. One could feel in prison in a palace, and Nuray knew why the white mansion was actually black. The color of the house came from the peace inside.

THIRTY-EIGHTH SCENE

Not knowing who your mother was like not knowing where you were born. There was a door into the world through which Reb had entered but she'd never known that door. She looked behind her and saw only emptiness. As she got older, the emptiness inside got bigger. She dreamed about a big door, and needed a mother figure whenever she needed that door. The mother on her mind was sometimes short and sometimes tall; overweight or thin; dark or blond, but she always looked like her mother. Whenever she looked back she saw a solid wall and no door.

Umah, Mirza's mother, was very nice to Reb. Reb looked for a job every day, and sometimes she found one for a short period of time, but never a permanent one. Mirza ran the pizza place, Hot Bite Pizza, with his father Idris. Idris was a quiet bearded strange man with white clothes.

Umah's daughter, Sadaf, also lived in San Francisco near the university. She was staying with her friend Lara and came home at weekends. Sadaf didn't like Reb. She was jealous of her as she had become the dear daughter of the house while Sadaf had been away. She saw Reb as a rival so she started visiting home more often.

Umah left twenty dollars in an envelope every day for Reb. At first Reb was very ashamed and tried to give it back, but in the end she couldn't resist Umah's persistence.

"When I find a permanent job, I'll pay all of it back."

THIRTY-EIGHTH SCENE

After three weeks in Mirza's home, Reb was sure that she couldn't live that way anymore. The night before, Sadaf had come to dinner and asked whether Reb was looking for a job or getting her own place. As she didn't have an answer to this question, Reb knew that her fears were coming true. She was falling down from the skies and the distance was great, although when she had been going up she hadn't thought so.

The streets were calling Reb; she didn't want to stay in this home anymore. It was five in the morning when she left a letter near Mariana's bed and left home. She went outside on tiptoes. The street was waiting for her just there.

The next morning, Umah found Mariana crying.

"Don't cry, my beauty, your mom will come home again soon."

Mirza memorized the letter Reb had left, but still read it again and again. His eyes filled with tears but he held them back. He threw the letter on the fire. He wanted to burn the words burning inside him that he couldn't speak out loud.

"Reb, come back immediately!"

THIRTY-NINTH SCENE

Cihan slammed the door of the car and winced as if the door had slammed in his face. First, he stumbled then he kicked the door. The car alarm went off. He quickly tried to stop it; he could stop the sirens outside, but he couldn't stop the ones inside. The noise in Cihan could be compared to the noise if all the car alarms in San Francisco had gone off at the same time.

These noises broke his glass, all the fragile parts of himself. What he had left were his rough parts.

He wanted to kick out and break something. To get rid of that feeling he would shake his head and get even deeper into chaos. What he was trying to get rid of was stuck to him, and every time he tried to get rid of it, it stuck to him even more. In his own chaos he walked up and down in the parking lot. Cihan had parked his car next to a van in the nearest spot to Pier 39. There were lots of cars on each floor and it was very hard to find a parking spot on a Saturday afternoon, but he was here before the dawn.

The day before he'd talked with Edom. He wanted to leave his car in the parking lot; he wanted to leave it as if it was his body and depart with his soul. However, it was only a parking lot for cars. How much would he pay to park his dead body?

He was all bullshit in this parking lot, the morning after a dark night. He was still drunk. Edom had called him at midnight.

"If you don't come here now, I'll jump off the bridge."

THIRTY-NINTH SCENE

Cihan had hurried to Golden Gate. He stepped on the gas, swearing at Edom and hitting the wheel.

"Enough, Edom, get out of my life! Breathe some other place, live without me. Find a new best friend. You have money, you are rich. Don't mess with me!"

He opened the window, swearing loudly, and when he saw a young same-sex couple walking hand in hand he put himself in their place. He wanted to push Edom off the bridge—Edom or himself. All he wanted was to end this suffering.

He parked his car and ran to the bridge but he couldn't see anybody on it. There was no one around except a few old homeless people.

Was it really possible that he was too late? He didn't want Edom to die, especially because of him.

"Please, God. Does he hate me enough to leave me with a lifetime of regret?"

It was 3.32 a.m. when Cihan arrived at the bridge. The wind was blowing, hitting his face and hurting Cihan. He wished he could only feel that pain, but the pain inside was so big that even the wind would be surprised. His heart was hitting him; he became blue with cold. He saw someone under a brown leather jacket laying down in the corner by the entrance. A handsome young man with a cool sports car was sleeping on the ground like a desperate homeless man.

"What do you want from me?"

Cihan didn't care about the tears on his cheeks. He surrendered completely and walked toward the man on the ground.

Edom pulled his jacket from his head. The look in his eyes was saying both come and go.

"Are you here?" He asked only to confirm what he saw. "Thanks."

"I'm here." Cihan bent down in front of Edom. "Why are you doing this to yourself? Okay, you don't care about yourself, so why are you doing this to me?"

Edom said everything without speaking. Cihan got lost in his silence. Finally he decided to sit down beside Edom, looking directly at the bridge.

"Are you going to jump from here? Damn, you'll hit a rock, you crazy!"

He was trying to cheer Edom up, but ended up feeling like a clown. Edom was still silent. His heart was beating in an almost dead body. Cihan put his hood back on his head and leaned over the handrail. The cold hurt him, but all of a sudden the pain left his body.

Edom put his head on Cihan's shoulders. Cihan didn't get mad; he was really calm. He would surrender to Edom no matter what he did. He laid all his weapons down, was surprised by himself. Could one call it pitying or heroism or fidelity?

He had known the owner of the head on his shoulder for years. Cihan was sure now that he was deep in curiosity. Edom didn't know that; all he knew was that Cihan was holding his hand now. It was a dark moment so it was still possible to destroy everything, but it was stupid to deny the truth. Cihan couldn't stop what was destined to happen. The future was holding a gun to his head and saying "Death or knot!" He hadn't chosen death, so Cihan found himself knotted.

★

Cihan was bringing Edom home. He turned on the car lights and turned off his own light. His world became dark, and San Francisco was very scary in this world. It was the last call to sin. Cihan didn't listen to it anymore. The night got dirty. Cihan was walking on the hair of life, and life was losing its hair and would become bald soon.

Cihan felt like he was cleaning paint from his face. It was the same color as the bridge, connecting him to the bridge, but there was no way out. He wanted to do something more extreme than death. He wanted to choke his curiosity. Cihan only said, "Why not?" The heart could carry most lies, but couldn't tolerate lying to itself. The human had two halves. The only thing that could make it whole was the opposite sex. When he put same sex pieces together, the entity would be still half.

What would he call himself and his dead body? He couldn't go home that way. In his home remained another Cihan, but he wasn't the same guy anymore.

He named himself with a black mark.

Edom wasn't the one to blame. Cihan had surrendered and became a slave to curiosity. What would happen now? The car was shaking like wine in an earthquake; he didn't have enough courage to keep driving. He parked his car on a parking lot and closed his eyes. His eyes closed him as well.

Alcatraz: The White Shirt with Five Holes

Lara realized that the white shirt she had wanted for two weeks was an absurd enthusiasm. This waiting made her forget to be happy. She had waited to buy it and now she had to wait to get rid of it. She didn't know where it was. Actually, what she didn't know was how to look for it.

There were lots of white shirts falling down from the sky, looking like parachutes. They appeared every morning and fell down to the ground with an invisible robe. The white shirts represented purity, cleanliness and freshness. The day was new. It was exciting that every living creature got to wear them. The new day was hot bread just out of the oven. A new and spotless twenty-four hours were in front of anyone with a white shirt.

The owners of these white shirts realized the shirts had five holes by the end of the day. Their souls were full of holes and they added five more each day. They knew how to patch things up, but they couldn't handle the holes in their shirts.

Every day this attack was repeated and the holes passed through to the souls. The emptiness caused by them couldn't be filled again and the cold was inside all the time.

FORTIETH SCENE

Nuray gave the purple lipstick to Michele as a present when she dropped the kids home.

"Thanks, I will wear it on Halloween."

One day Nuray saw Michele with the white guy again. She closed the curtains as a sign of disapproval, but her curiosity was piqued so she watched them from behind the curtains. Michele was happy, Nuray was sure, but she couldn't understand why she was still with her husband.

She activated the vacuum cleaner again. Sometimes the noises inside her were so loud that she wanted to suppress them with a louder noise, namely the vacuum. Even though it made her back hurt, she vacuumed the room more than necessary.

"Let's see how the story will end. Sooner or later Robert will hear that his wife is cheating on him."

She went into the kitchen and filled a glass with water.

"I am becoming just like the tailor Melahat in the village. She used to talk to herself. Am I getting too old?"

Everyone morning Nuray prepared a pot of Turkish tea. For the last twenty-five years, whenever she went to Turkey she had spoken about how she was amazed at Americans drinking coffee before eating anything. One day that would happen to her too, but she hadn't known it then.

She made some coffee. Black Turkish coffee. She was being American, but keeping her Turkish side. She waited beside the coffeepot and saw the note on the fridge. She had memorized it, but she believed that while she was reading it she was losing weight.

"Breakfast 300 calories, lunch 400 calories, dinner 500 calories."

There was Jessica Alba's photo under this note. Nobody else would say she looked after herself, but Nuray thought she was losing weight. The photo and numbers were supposed to make her eat less, but it wasn't possible. Whenever she tried to discipline herself to eat less, she ended up eating more. She made promises to herself that tomorrow she would begin her diet, but she knew she wouldn't.

Sabahat was still in her room, sleeping. When she first came to America, her son-in-law had told her she could be jetlagged, but she hadn't understood what that foreign word meant. It wasn't jetlag but concern about Nuray that caused her insomnia, and now she was concerned about her grandson Cihan.

*

Lara opened her wardrobe and looked for a thick jumper. She was an untidy person; she found red shorts, thin socks, her new T-shirt, a bag—everything except something warm.

She took the bag with *Inci Market* written on it and thought while looking at it. When had she bought it? What was inside? What had she eaten that day? Did she use her credit card or cash?

She didn't know what to do with it; she wanted to go where it belonged. "You wouldn't be sad, little girl, if you could get rid of yourself," she said, leaving her room.

Lara put Marcy's catalog in her bag and left home. This time she didn't insist on Sadaf coming with her. She wanted to be on her own, but she wasn't able to stay alone for a long time. She entered

FORTIETH SCENE

the store and looked around aimlessly, feeling it was compulsory to buy something. She didn't like this side of herself. She had a lot of things she didn't use that she had bought in sales. After buying the things, she lost interest in them, and that was what she didn't like.

When she'd met a woman who gave everything to the man she loved and waited ten years for him, she had realized the difference between wanting and having. Once she possessed what she desired, she may think that nothing would be the same. But actually nothing would change. Looking for it, wanting it, trying to get it were the keywords of life, but sometimes what you were looking for was not in the same place as what you wanted.

Lara purchased the shirt and realized that shopping was the last drop of her love. She might have said it was the last drop every time she shopped, but she always went back to the start.

"The homesickness is like an arrow in my heart. Everything is foreign to me."

They were the lyrics to the song she was listening to in the car. Lara had put in the CD her mother had given to her by mistake. It was quite strange to listen to a Turkish song after all this time.

"Everything is foreign to me," Lara repeated. The lyrics hurt her. She didn't know whether to cry or laugh as she pitied herself.

The train of homesickness had arrived in her station.

"Turkey, you are missed by someone. Are you aware of that?"

Lara shouted, but only she heard what she said. It was that low, but loud enough to break the windows of the train of homesickness.

Lara threw her shopping bags on the sofa and turned her laptop on. There were no emails. She read and sent the email she had written two days ago but forgotten to send.

*

Hello, my dear (Tuesday 04.13 a.m.)

Today I had soup at Fisherman's Wharf. The soup was delicious, but different as they put it inside the bread. Meltem took me there. You know, she is the daughter of Aunt Nuray. I stayed with her when I first came here. She is so skinny, dark and tall. She is a little jealous, but nice.

This city is like Istiklal Street. Yasemin. We used to sit and watch people with Cüneyt and Sezgi. remember? There were all kinds of people, just like the U.S.A. It's like Istiklal Street got bigger and became the U.S. Isn't it funny, a fat street?

Here old people don't retire. They do all their jobs themselves. There is a radio station and a programmer has a show there, but she must be at least eighty years old. They keep driving even though they are shaking. I can't think of my grandma driving ☺ and the traffic is even worse than Istanbul—okay, I might exaggerate a little, but sometimes it is unbearable. Some roads are too steep. Sometimes I can't help wondering how anyone can live at the top of some of the hills. If it snows, you can ski on some streets—not a bad idea, right? Joking aside, here is too far away. You are too far away; all my loved ones are far away. Everywhere and everything is too far!

Where am I? Who are they? Okay, they are strangers, but am I a stranger to myself?

I'm uncomfortable in my own skin and getting lonelier.

Well, how are you? Are you happy?

Lara.

FORTY-FIRST SCENE

Cihan examined himself after having shaved and pulled out the remaining small hairs. He put on his aftershave from the horse-figure bottle, but he felt he still smelled bad. His moral compass wasn't right and this made him a bad-smelling person..

Cihan was not in love with Edom, he was just trying himself out. He didn't identify himself as Edom did. While he was still in doubt, Edom had promised to take him from his chaos.

"I didn't reject him, it was just unresponsiveness," he said to himself. He hated himself more and more, but lost his senses in the end.

He had seen his life story while looking in the mirror. Their childhood wasn't over yet; the things they were doing were just childhood misbehaviors. This behavior may hurt them, but they could forget it as it was done in childhood. They fooled themselves as a mother fooled her child by hitting the chair that the kid had crashed into. The chair didn't know or mind, and Cihan wasn't sure what he was doing either.

Edom was more concerned than Cihan. He had a constant fear of being dumped. They didn't walk on the street together; they did nothing together except at home. That was why Edom began feeling like he was at home when on the street and on the street when he was at home.

Alcatraz: Bicycle

Lara couldn't believe her eyes. She closed them and opened them again, but the prisoners were still naked.

When people took off their clothes, when their body homes became more visible, they became the targets of strangers' eyes as a result. They were hurt by lots of eyeshot. They were defenseless. They declared their independence under a flag of freedom, but it was actually a declaration of dependence. Nobody was able to see the ball and chain of their soul. They took off everything on them. Their skin became their prison clothing. The roads, mountains, birds were ashamed, but they were not.

What they presumed was not real. The things you didn't hide didn't belong to you. Their bodies denied their existence. When an avalanche fell down on them, the bodies weren't able to hear their screams.

If you got kicked out of your own body house, you would be homeless in this world till you freed yourself from the prison.

FORTY-SECOND SCENE

"Meltem, can you hurry please? I am putting down roots here." She opened her arms and reached out to the sky like a tree.

"Okay, I'm coming," said Meltem for the third time.

Lara was restless while she was zipping up her black and white sports jacket. She opened her arms again, inhaling deeply. She felt like she was suffocating inside so she liked being outside. Maybe her mother had been right, saying that she needed to come back. After the death of her father, Lara had become even more restless. She always wanted a change.

She put on her hair band and headphones again.

"I'm out of here, Meltem!"

Meltem picked up her bag covered in pins of peace and love and followed Lara. She put on a fake smile to calm Lara down.

"Let's go, follow me. The roads are a bit complex here, you could get lost."

"Don't worry, honey. I walk every morning, I know my way."

Meltem put her bag in the basket on the front of her bicycle and drank some water. They both waited for the cars to pass before beginning their journey. When they finally started pedaling, they got faster and faster.

"You don't walk around here, so you'd better follow me. It is not as steep as here around the campus."

"Okay, honey. I'm following you, no worries."

Meltem cycled toward Lara and almost crushed her.

"Are you crazy? That's not funny at all, you nearly made me fall off."

Meltem stopped under a big tree with white flowers. Her phone was ringing.

"Hi, Cihan! Well, we are at…I was wandering around San Francisco with Lara, and Mom is now with us. She's taking Emir to see a doctor. Yes, Mom talked with her this morning. The air conditioner made her a little dizzy, but she is okay. Bye!"

"Aunt Sabahat is back in Turkey? I thought she would be here for a few weeks more. I wanted to say goodbye."

"Yes, she left yesterday. There is a wedding in her village, she wants to be there."

Lara was looking around.

"No stopping, let's move!"

"It's quite a big park. Looks like Yıldız Park in Istanbul."

Lara wanted to liken every place to Istanbul to feel as if she was home. She wished Yasemin was with her, but her fiancé didn't let her travel. He didn't want to be away from her even for a moment.

Lara wished she'd had someone to tell her not to go.

*

Lara and Meltem had said goodbye and Lara was going home. When she arrived on Market Street and Embarcadero it was 12.40. There were crowds of people running with their cameras, screaming. Lara was tall, but she couldn't see what was happening.

FORTY-SECOND SCENE

There was some loud applause and Lara got even more curious. While she was pushing her way to the front, she heard strange conversations all around.

"Hey, have you seen his thing?"

"I don't think fat people should be naked. They look terrible."

"I don't mind, it's freedom!"

There were hundreds of bikes on the street and the riders were all naked. Lara couldn't believe her eyes. These people had enough courage to become the focus of hundreds of eyes. She wanted to look away but couldn't, so she felt ashamed.

A TV Channel was interviewing a naked woman and Lara listened to the conversation.

"Everybody is looking at you. What do you think about that?"

"We are here to be seen, but to be honest I sometimes feel like an animal in a cage. Especially when they stare at us."

"Are you comfortable with being seen and photographed like this?"

"I wasn't that comfortable last year as it was quite strange. This year, I came here drunk so I am comfortable enough. Yes, I am comfortable. That's life."

FORTY-THIRD SCENE

She was trying to tear a piece off the new toilet paper, but it wasn't tearing through the perforations. While trying to put it right, she'd had to tear a lot of pieces. She was fighting with the toilet paper. The entire incident was like her emotional life.

She washed her hands and left the toilet. It was her seventh week on the street and she missed Mariana a lot. The money Umah had given her was used up in the first week. She hoped to find a job and a new home soon as her only concern was to get Mariana back, but whenever she applied she got rejected as she didn't have a permanent address and phone number.

She went to a dinner given by a church two days ago. The priest she'd met there had told her she could give his name and address when applying for jobs, which made Reb very happy. She didn't really have trouble finding food; she waited in front of restaurants and finished the food of customers who weren't able to eat everything on their plates. Leftovers became her feast. She remembered back to her childhood when she had got angry with a friend who drank cola from her glass. Now she was eating from strangers' plates without any concern for hygiene.

Reb was waiting in front of a restaurant on Castro Street, looking more like a model than homeless in her black pants, cream jacket and cream boots.

"Reb! Reb!"

FORTY-THIRD SCENE

She froze. She couldn't move and didn't dare turn round. A hand touched her shoulder and she had to turn round. It was Sadaf, and she was the most warmhearted person Reb had seen in weeks. Strangely, when they had spent weekends together at Mirza's house, Reb had only seen her with a long face. Sadaf had never smiled at Reb; her face used to scream "Go away!" at her. Now, that same face was smiling at her.

Sadaf was very excited to see Reb, whom all her family missed. Unexpectedly, she hugged Reb.

"Please come back home, Reb. Mariana and my mom are very sad."

She held out her hands, but Reb withdrew.

"Thanks, Sadaf. Say hi to Umah, but I can't go back. I don't want to live like a parasite, I want to stand on my own two feet."

"Okay, I see, but Mirza is very worried about you."

"Tell him not to worry, I'm okay."

"Where do you live? Do you have any money?"

Reb pretended not to have heard what Sadaf said. She covered her face and ran off, fast.

"Stop! Please wait! Stop!"

Reb ran into a woman with long braids and big breasts.

"Be careful!" she said in a very deep voice. When she saw Reb was crying, she held up her hands.

"Okay, no problem."

Reb stopped in front of a liquor shop. Her heart was beating very fast; she wondered why she was so excited. Reb wouldn't ever have told Sadaf she was living on the street, but she was sure Sadaf knew anyway. It hurt that Sadaf felt sorry for her and that was the reason she had asked her to come home. Reb hated feeling sorry for herself, but now she was doing what she hated because of Sadaf.

★

Sadaf decided not to follow Reb and got on a bus home. Actually she had been going to the house she shared with Lara, but she decided not to after having seen Reb. She had to tell her mom what had happened; Mirza would be so relieved. She wasn't a hundred percent sure whether to tell Mirza, though; maybe not telling him would be better.

How she could she tell Mirza that Reb was okay when she believed Reb was living on the street? Saying nothing would be better, but it would be very hard for her to pretend nothing had happened. She had never been able to do this. The news was important, but she was unable to decide whether it was good or bad news. The journey passed quickly as she thought things over.

"Why are you here, Sadaf? I thought you had papers to write. You didn't tell me you were coming. Such a nice surprise at dinner time. Let me hug you!"

"I'm going upstairs to wash my face. Then I'll be back."

Sadaf walked to Mirza's room. She was sure he had forgotten the pain in his legs while suffering such heartache. She had thought about being extra careful while talking to him, but as soon as she was in his room she began right away.

"Do you know who I saw today?"

She had entered the room in such excitement it would be awkward to say she had seen anyone else. But then she had decided not to say, so she would tell some other story and explain her excitement as being because she missed him.

"Reb!"

The truth came out unexpectedly. When Mirza heard Reb's name, he immediately turned round and faced Sadaf.

"Where? When? How? Is she here, *baji* Sadaf?"

FORTY-THIRD SCENE

"Not now, but she will be."

Mirza lay back on his bed and pulled a sour face.

"Waiting is like death, *baji* Sadaf."

"I know."

"How do you know? Who are you waiting for?"

FORTY-FOURTH SCENE

"Meltem, what's wrong with you?"
"Nothing, Mom. Can you please leave my room?"

"No, I will not till you tell me what has happened to you. You are awake all night and go to school like a drunken person. You are angry all the time. Okay, your grades are better, but you are worse than ever. Are you in love? Tell your mama."

"No, Mom, I'm addicted to drugs."

Nuray felt like she had smashed into glass without knowing it was there. She froze at her daughter's bedside.

"What did you say?"

"I said I'm addicted, in a very bad way. I'm using drugs."

"Where do you get them?"

"I don't get them, they are already here. Adderall, Emir's ADHD drug, but sometimes I use Ritalin. I exchange whatever I can find with friends. You spoke to the child psychiatrist and decided not to use the drugs, so I used them. "

"Why, Meltem? Why?"

"Mom, think about it. Your brain works a lot faster. I heard from friends that college students use it for academic success. I tried it and got As in my exams, so I continued."

FORTY-FOURTH SCENE

Nuray was devastated. The drugs they had got for Emir to make him better had instead made their daughter sick.

"They make me feel and work better."

Nuray wasn't able to hear Meltem anymore, or she was able to hear but not understand. When she had first come to the U.S.A., she had been like that: choosing every word to say in a language she didn't know.

"Mom, please do not ask any questions. I'm not in the mood for talking, I have an exam tomorrow."

Nuray didn't say anything. She went out of the room like a robot, moving slowly as if she had lost all her power.

She found Şahin watching a boxing match.

"Come on, boy, kick him! Faster, go!"

She crept up to him and began talking.

"Our daughter is addicted to drugs. She is academically successful, but addicted. Are you happy now?"

"What are you talking about, Nuray? Are you crazy?"

"Not me, you are the one who is crazy. You made our daughter go mad all by yourself."

She went to the computer, searched for 'Adderall high dose' on the Internet and began reading the articles on the websites.

Şahin ran upstairs in three bounds and knocked on Meltem's door.

"Please open the door, Meltem. Tell me, is your mom telling the truth? Is it true what I have heard?"

He knocked on the door again and again.

"Meltem, open the door, please. I won't get mad."

★

At breakfast no one was happy. The emotional earthquake that had happened the previous night had left debris on the table. Meltem didn't even go downstairs for breakfast. Şahin tried to get Cihan's cooperation, but he was not in a cooperative mood.

"Cihan, school is over now for you. I've handed your CV to my boss and he liked it a lot. He is going to introduce you to someone."

"Okay, Dad. Bon appétit!"

"You'll get a good job, then find a good wife."

"Don't talk to me about marriage!"

"How can you say such a thing? I'm your father!"

"Okay, Father, but there are thing you don't know about."

"What?"

Cihan was silent; he decided to talk with his silence.

Nuray was still looking for a lemon since Şahin wanted some for his soup.

"Are you picking lemons from the trees, Nuray? Come to the table, your soup's getting cold."

"The reason is lemon."

Cihan walked toward to door.

Nuray had been pretending to look for a lemon in the kitchen as she was sure they would change the subject when she came to the table.

"I've found the lemon, I've been looking for something else."

She returned to the table with salt.

"Where is the lemon?"

"Oh, I forgot it."

The door opened and Cihan went outside. Then he craned his neck back through the door.

FORTY-FOURTH SCENE

"I am together with Edom. I don't know how you will handle this, but stop trying to get me married off. I'm happy this way."

Şahin stopped chewing his food; he had to cough. Nuray sat on the floor; Şahin helped her stand up and sat her on the chair. Cihan didn't want to hear their comments so he just told the truth and left the scene. He wanted to close the door behind himself without any reaction from anyone.

"*Vuun vuun, duut biiiiip!*" The only sound was from Emir, who was playing with his cars.

Nuray was wearing her black velvet headband, but it was about to fall from her head. Her hair had turned white to the roots. Her life was turning white too, from the white of her wedding dress to her burial robe.

"These children will be the death of me while I'm still healthy."

Nuray remembered her mother complaining and now she was doing the same. Then she remembered her grandmother Şukufe's words:

"Daughters finally turn into their mothers."

What about sons?

*

Şahin hadn't been able to eat for three days. He wasn't an angry and cold man anymore. In contrast to his old self, he became fragile and naïve. His despair was huge. Nuray and Şahin felt they had failed as parents.

The bombs had exploded consecutively. First Meltem's drug addiction then Cihan's relationship with Edom. As a result, Şahin had to work from home and Nuray locked herself in her bedroom with the curtains closed. She refused light and gave herself to darkness.

Cihan moved in with Edom. Nuray and Şahin had known Edom since childhood, calling him the rich blond Jew. He had been a silent child, so they would never have guessed things would turn out like this.

Nuray had actually had a feeling, but she never asked Cihan. Her mother kept calling her to arrange a marriage for Cihan, but Nuray knew he would never accept that. Cihan was a hard and peremptory man, and when he got angry he could be very offensive.

The door slammed in the wind. Even though the door was closed, the freezing wind was whistling around. It was time for regrets. Nuray and Şahin had lost two of their children and were unable to find a solution.

"What are we going to do, darling?"

Şahin called Nuray darling maybe for the first time ever. Nuray closed her eyes and felt like she had her maroon lipstick on. She licked her lips.

"Nuray, are you okay?"

Nuray woke up from her dream.

"Okay? No."

"Were we sleeping when Cihan and Meltem went in the wrong direction?"

Şahin shook her, holding her shoulders.

"Dad, don't fight Mom!"

Emir ran to his mother and hugged her.

"Nothing is wrong, Emir." She caressed his head. "We'll talk later."

Nuray took Emir's hand and walked to the living room. There was nothing to talk about later; there was no later.

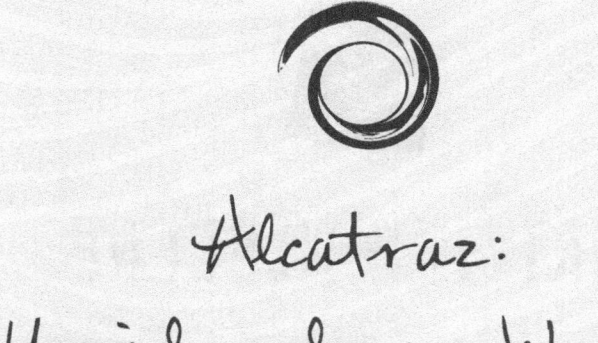

Alcatraz: Upside-down World

Lara was putting bars on the window of her heart to complete the view in her mind. She looked behind the bars, pouring concrete on the feet of her looks. She ignored the ones demolishing the wall before her eyes because she was applauding the ones building the walls. Everything was upside-down. Lara would have put it right if she had known how to.

Homes rising from the ground clung to the roofs raining from the sky. The roof was upside-down so lives hung in the air. People had to walk upside-down to live in these homes or demolish them and build new ones.

In the world of upside-down souls, trees hung from the skies and stars gazed from the ground. One had to climb to the stars to go from one place to another.

Lara tried to walk upside-down in her upside-down world. She wasn't successful though. She realized that changing herself was more difficult than changing the world.

FORTY-FIFTH SCENE

Lara seemed a little older in her white shirt, brown pants and pastel makeup. She began talking with confidence, looking at the faces in the conference room. She was speaking non-stop about homeless people to the curious audience, then she stopped abruptly as she saw someone entering the room.

Lara looked at the audience, and they were looking curiously at her as no one understood why she had stopped talking. She began her presentation again, but she stuttered then went silent.

She was not going to be able to continue like this.

"Everyone, I'd like you to turn your attention to our guest. My hero, right there."

She pointed at Johnson.

"And now, if he wants, I would like to invite him to the stage."

She got Professor Richard's approval.

"We are waiting for you, Johnson, please."

She opened her arms as if she was going to hug him.

There was loud applause in the conference room. Johnson stood up and put his hand on his heart. He bowed to thank the audience for the applause, but he didn't come to the stage.

"Okay, then I have nothing more to say. I cannot talk about homelessness in front of a homeless man."

FORTY-FIFTH SCENE

Lara left the stage and began packing her things into her bag. Johnson came to her and whispered in her ear.

"I think I can do it."

"Of course you can."

Lara nearly fainted from happiness and excitement. There was no sound to be heard in the conference room. Lara sat down on the chair next to Professor Richard, wondering very much what Johnson would say. She had only said, "It would be very nice if you'd come to the presentation tomorrow and tell us your story," but she had neither asked if he would nor insisted. She had only wished. Johnson had asked her the time of the lecture, but had avoided any more questions. Lara hadn't been expecting him; that he had come was a huge surprise.

Johnson blew into the microphone; he still had doubts about talking. He squinted his left eye; he wasn't able to see the audience in the distance. He took the microphone and walked on the stage feeling like he was eighty years old. Sitting cross-legged on the stage, he pulled up his pants which made his dirty white sneakers stand out. He pulled his hair back and suddenly began talking in a loud voice.

"Isn't it strange to be on the streets?"

His voice echoed in the room, startling the students, pushing them like a strong wind. Sometimes the way things were said could praise the words or made them garbage.

Johnson continued calmly as he had been preparing for his speech for a long time. He was looking directly at people's faces, confidently giving his monologue. After a while he put on his white baseball hat and went on speaking in a lower voice, as if talking to his dog, Joe.

"I know what it is like to live in a house, but you have no idea about living on the streets. That's why the topic is so strange to you. Don't tell me that you did camp or stayed in the mountains. Staying on the streets of a city is way harder than staying in nature. Why am I on the streets? Not because I have no home, but because I accept the streets as my home. This is my own choice: my home is my street. You may not believe it, but I am happy this way."

He answered everyone's questions as if reading their minds. Instead of telling his story, he was following a path of unanswered questions.

"You may think of us as alcoholics, uneducated and useless. This is quite wrong. There are some homeless who used to rank very highly in society, then they lost everything. Some do not even call themselves homeless. As for me, I can't deny I have drunk a lot. I have also been involved in bodily injury and robbery cases. I was in prison for a while, for a short time did drugs. However I managed to free myself from the things that made me dependent.

"Hey, you! The one with the glasses sitting in the middle—yes, the one asking 'Me?' Do you know that it is not the same for you to open a pizza box as it is for me? You only open a box, while I open a treasure chest.

"Some of you call us 'shadow people'. You are real and we are just your shadows. Really? You are very wrong. I'm homeless and I'm aware of that. I'm here with all my awareness. You have homes, but you remain homeless and you die without even realizing it. What about it? If you don't know which street your doors open onto, you are the real shadow people. Homelessness without awareness is much more dangerous, believe it or not.

"We are known, accepted. We are who we are. We don't have a roof above our heads, but what about your upside down roofs, relationships and worlds? Who can call them home? We are the residents of the streets, but you do not even belong to the streets because you have closed your doors on both sides. You are stuck between the inside and outside; you live in emptiness.

FORTY-FIFTH SCENE

"I am homeless, right? And I am well aware of that, but you? Where is your home? I am the visible homeless, you are the invisible ones. That is the difference between us. You are the real homeless, not me. Now please, you, namely the real homeless people, come to the stage as I'm going home."

He left the microphone and took a scroll from his belt. It was a yellow rag and the words were black. While he held it up to the audience, they tried to read what was written on it.

You are without HOME or YOU are HOME.

Johnson put the rag in his pocket and didn't care about the rest of his speech. He jumped from the stage and flew to the exit.

Lara froze, doing nothing but watching his exit. Then she applauded and the whole room joined her. Everybody was on their feet, applauding heavily.

"Thanks for listening!"

Lara took her bag and followed Johnson. She couldn't find him anywhere, though. Lara realized she would actually become homeless from that moment on. Nothing and no country could calm her down. Because of Johnson she had no peace. In the end she couldn't call anywhere home.

When one burned oneself, the first scream would be loud, but the pain would become worse after a while. However, by then one wouldn't be screaming, only living one's own pain in silence. Real pain was lived in silence.

She wasn't on the streets, but actually she was. She had a home, but actually she didn't. In her daydream, Lara put herself on the stage as a homeless person.

FORTY-SIXTH SCENE

It had been eight months since Nuray noticed her neighbor Michele was cheating on her husband. The guy came two times a week now instead of three times as before. Nuray knew when he came—on Wednesdays and Fridays—as she picked up the twins from the school.

The morning of January 27 was different than every other day. Nuray went to the Mail Office to send some medication to her mother and father. She saw her neighbor Robert as she was standing in line. She didn't want to talk to him so she was praying that the other mail officer would take her parcel. Squeezing the parcel, she looked back and saw seven people behind. She wanted to stay where she was, but unfortunately for her she had to go to Robert's desk.

"Hi, Nuray, how are you?"

Nuray was trying hard to avoid any eye contact.

"Your mail is for Turkey, right?"

"Yes."

Robert wasn't able to hear her as she couldn't even hear herself. Nuray coughed, trying to imply there was a problem with her throat.

"Yes."

"Where is our baklava? You promised to bake some for us."

FORTY-SIXTH SCENE

"Oh, I completely forgot about it. I'll bake some for you today." Nuray leaned over the desk and whispered, "When is your lunch break?"

"In half an hour. Why do you ask?"

"I need to talk to you about something."

"Okay, I will talk to the manager and see if I can come now. Wait for me."

Another mail officer took over from Robert and Nuray panicked. *What I have done?* She had thought she would be giving Robert a gift by telling him what she knew.

Robert opened the door to the garden for her and showed her to a bench. Nuray felt scared and shy. She put on her navy-blue headband again and took a deep breath.

"Well, I don't know how to say this, but Michele..."

"Michele is cheating on me?"

A chill ran down on Nuray's back.

"Wait a minute, you already know?"

"Nuray, we have an open marriage. We made a deal before we got married: we can have lovers occasionally. We let each other do so."

"What do you mean by letting? Why did you get married in the first place then? How about the twins?"

"We don't lie to each other. We are free to do anything. I had someone last month, but we didn't come home. You know, I'm quite busy."

"Okay, don't continue, please! It's just something I'm not used to. I wanted to warn you, but you already...whatever."

"Are you okay?"

Nuray was about to faint. She felt disgusted with Michele and Robert. Nuray told him to go with hand gestures and walked to the car. What she had heard was worse then what she had seen. The world's biggest vacuum wouldn't be able to drown out the noise in her now.

Marriage was meant to be a shelter, a way to say no to all other people. Marriage was meant to be a journey into peace, but Michele and Robert were sharing their bedroom with a whole city. Their home was transparent, without a roof, just like their relationship. Their truth was a lie, and Nuray decided not to associate with them anymore. She had to buy a black lipstick for Michele, because today was as dark as coal.

★

Nuray was looking at the seagulls on the seashore. Her mother had called to tell her that Grandma Şukufe had died. Life was very strange. Her mother had gone home for a wedding but had ended up at a funeral. Hearing the bad news so far away had its own bad sides as Nuray felt trapped in a foreign country. Going home would take as long as fifteen hours, and there were not many flights. Losing loved ones from afar made even near places become distant.

She called Şahin immediately.

"I feel so bad, come home."

"I can't leave work right now. It will take some time. If home was near, I would come, believe me."

"I would go to Turkey, if it was near."

Nuray's dreams were lying shattered on a sad and hurt sea shore. She was trapped by water like Alcatraz. The guy she loved had made her a prisoner in the middle of water. There was no land to be seen; her love for him was deep inside Alcatraz and she knew it didn't have much time left.

FORTY-SIXTH SCENE

Nuray had to go home but her feet had lost their power. Her inner woman escaped from prison and told her, "Your husband is cheating on you and you are still living in that home. There is someone in your heart who treats you like a second-class citizen. How can you live like that? Go away! Go, go, go!"

Going was acceptance and confirmation. Going was defeat, losing a war before it had even started. But staying and resisting were trouble. Dark trouble. Nuray was light.

Meltem and Cihan were grownups now, but what about Emir? Was it right to take him away from his dad and force him to live in Konya? She had been living in this country for twenty-five years and still felt like a stranger. Would Emir feel the same in Turkey?

No matter the color of your skin you are human, and the only thing that matters is the color of your heart. She was going to book her ticket home. There was no use changing her mind; she needed her soul to take off.

*

The plane took off at 6.30. Nuray put her love in Alcatraz and made her husband its guardian. If he let it go, then it would be free. Would she live in prison all her life or be freed by Şahin? Up in the plane, her thoughts became grounded. She knew Turkey would make her better.

"Mom, will you let me play with cat Mom, she won't hurt me. I'll be careful, please!"

"Okay, you be careful, then."

She closed her eyes as if she could make the truth disappear. She wanted to take a breath of fresh air by opening the windows of the plane. Her mind was looking for an escape route; there was none, though.

"I am as lonely as the stars in the sky."

Luckily she had Emir, her little one. Motherhood was hard, and she was afraid of losing her happiness. What if something bad happened to her son? What if he fell from the balcony? All the bad things came into her mind after being thankful for having him.

The journey was long; she needed to have some sleep, but first she had to put her feelings to sleep. Emir was already asleep; she wanted to be in his place. She was calling sleep to take her, yet she had so much on her mind. She knew what had held Şahin this long was the kids. If a child is sleeping on your knees, you cannot move.

Motherhood was the next stop of being a woman, and womanhood was the last mansion one stayed in before motherhood. The mansion had been sold long before, and the woman of the home was crying in the kitchen even though she wasn't chopping an onion. Without seeing the whole picture, knowing that her husband was cheating on her and that the other woman was beautiful, she was not able to leave that easily.

"You have a baby in your lap so you will be called by another name till your death. Go home and chop onions so you have a reason to cry. Let your tears out, but don't tell anyone. You can't leave this man. This command is from the sky."

She was flying like a plane on the plane, which made the cabin pressure unbearable. She was angry and looked down; her orange juice had spilled on the ground.

There was a small plane on the world map.

Arrival will be in seven hours forty-seven minutes.

She had been flying for a long time, yet she still had a long way to go.

FORTY-SEVENTH SCENE

Reb went to Hoer Burgers as soon as she heard they were looking for a waitress. The woman at the cashier desk handed her a form to fill out, and she gave the name and address of the priest.

The owner was mid-height, a little overweight; a white American with long hair. She didn't ask anything and gave Reb an apron.

"Start immediately."

Reb was crying from happiness. To hide her tears she ran to the kitchen.

"This is how you make the bread." The owner carried on talking non-stop, not giving Reb a chance to say anything.

*

It had been fifteen days since Reb started her job. There was no bed in the shelter near the restaurant so she had to go to Oakland every day. It was hard to stay on the streets when she had a job; she had to take a shower every day, which meant waiting at least two hours in line. One night an old woman started a fight in the bedroom so Reb couldn't sleep, and when she finally did she overslept and missed her bus. When she got to her job it was only to learn that she had been fired.

She never liked the streets and the streets never liked her.

FORTY-EIGHTH SCENE

The red bridge was foggy and windy again. Cihan was walking between people fishing and those picnicking. The dance of the grass was carrying the conversation in green. The kites and the people controlling them were up in the blue.

The pictures of the city became different in Cihan's mind. He didn't know where he had put the images.

Children were playing ball games. They had something to play, but Cihan had nothing left. He and Edom used to play on this grass and the grass used to be green and long, but now they were stepped on and had become a path. Cihan was attending the funeral of his childhood.

Who could stop a train coming at full speed with one hand?

If he could select the sides he didn't like about himself, only a little would remain. He couldn't call this life.

He remembered the note on Edom's fridge:

While you are walking on the road, sometimes it flies like a magic carpet and you go up high with it, then roll inside it. Do you have enough power to be yourself? If not, fly away.

Cihan was surfing on the ocean of complicated thoughts and was tired of falling in. He had got into his car and driven to the red bridge, thinking about the people on it. How many of them were thinking about jumping off?

FORTY-EIGHTH SCENE

He had to silence his mind. He had never liked uncontrolled ideas. He was afraid of himself as uncontrolled thoughts made him blind.

There were phones on Golden Gate Bridge for emergencies. They were also used for the last goodbyes of those committing suicide. Leaving with sound hurt people more. Saying goodbye before death was important. The ones left behind knew when the voice had gone, they were gone.

The feelings were screams.

"I can't hear."

"Alo!"

*

Being on the balcony was neither inside nor outside. Maybe it was both. You weren't able to see inside when you were completely outside, so feeling the need to have one foot inside was essential. There had to be something supporting the balcony or you would fall down.

Cihan was standing on the balcony. He had met his monster on it and it had made fun of him. Cihan was listening metal music; the electric guitar was scratching like metal inside him. The higher the volume went, the bigger the monster got. The childish side of Cihan began running behind him. He didn't know whether to run away or hug him. If there was someone running behind him, he couldn't be standing still. Yet he was there, not moving, so the running child must have been in another dimension. There was a war happening inside him, messing up his mind.

Cihan was watching the view from the room he stayed in with Edom. Many people admired the view of the bridge at night, yet it was hurting him.

Edom was at a business dinner with his father, so Cihan was alone at home, watching the view of Golden Gate from their window without curtains. There were a lot of curtains in Cihan's soul, though. They were made from velvet and opened by a machine that he had no control over.

The night made the waters into a nightmare. There was a man crying on a small balcony in Sausalito. Cihan's family knew he was with Edom, yet he didn't want to admit it to himself. Some of the pieces were missing in the puzzle.

The lyrics began: *Why, but why, but why?*

He had regrets all because of that red bridge. The music stopped. The night was over. Cihan began watching his soul on the balcony of his mind.

FORTY-NINTH SCENE

When Johnson had learned of his father's death from the neighbors he had run to the tree in the garden. Mark had built him a tree house to cover his sin. By building the house he would prove his innocence and how much he liked Johnson. The tree house was a huge lie, but they hugged each other anyway. The tree was hard, a human was soft, so they completed each other. The tree was like a father that didn't respond to his hugging child.

Waiting for but never getting his desires, he aimed at not waiting at all. Never was always with him, but always was always away.

*

Once in street prison, Johnson didn't know whether he was living in the handcuffs of freedom as the street had made him its inmate. The street was sometimes a guardian, sometimes an angry father. Johnson wanted to shelter behind the fatherly side of the street but had got slapped by it. Even though it might embrace him, the fatherly side could be more pitiless than the guardian side.

Johnson barely remembered the face of his car mechanic father. He tried very hard to forget his face, but sometimes he needed to look at that picture. That was why he had stored his father's picture in his mind drawer. His father had burned half of his face while welding. Johnson had at first been very scared of his face, and then had got used to it as his behavior was way worse.

He remembered the times when he was in the dark room in the garage. Even though he was thirty years old now, he was still scared of garages. They always reminded him of captivity within freedom. One cold day a man had invited him to sleep in his garage and Johnson had beaten him very badly. That was why he had gone to prison.

Johnson learned the bitter truth a week after his escape from home. Julie had got into the car her husband was fixing without being seen and had run over him. She went to prison and was sentenced to life, and Mark was dead.

This story led Johnson to live on the light streets instead of in the dark houses.

FIFTIETH SCENE

Rannan Mandel was watching the chaotic face of the city from the window of his white mansion on Broadway Street. The wrinkles on his face resembled the city's wavelike roads. One could sometimes see a city on the face of a person.

There was a floor-to-ceiling bookshelf and next to it a tall purple lamp. The light coming from that lamp was reflecting on the oil painting. Inside the golden mirror there was a man, a city and sadness. The lights of the bridge collided with the lights of the house. Everything stable seemed to be moving. The houses seemed to be passing the bridge or the cars were about to enter the house. The pictures changed places in his mind.

He took a sip from his coffee and left the flowered porcelain cup on the antique console.

Kate was lying on the cream velvet sofa, completely focused on a home decoration magazine. She looked at ice-blue and white lampshades and a white sofa with blue flowers. She imagined a white fireplace, a brown sofa and ice-blue rug in the room. Turning the page, she focused on a bedroom with bone colored bed, cream sheets, big brown candlesticks and books on the coffee table. It was time for the kitchen to change when she turned another page. She looked at a picture of two green olives and kashar cheese and realized that she was hungry.

"Do you need anything, madam?"

Kate came back to the real world at Maya's voice. Contrary to her baby voice, Maya was a dark, hairy and manly woman.

"A fruit salad, please, but I want lots of pineapple in it, and strawberry sauce and walnuts on it."

She didn't even look up from the magazine as she had pre-prepared her order.

"Yes, madam. What about you, sir?"

"Another coffee, please."

The two people had been sitting in the big living room for the last two hours without talking to each other. Rannan Mandel had been worrying about the outside world while Kate was reading magazines. They were like inanimate objects till Maya had come in.

Rannan sat beside Kate. He looked very noble in his white thin-striped shirt and black sweater.

"Kate, I'm going to Israel. I will live there for a while to plan the new chocolate factory. You can go anywhere you want. You can move to your mother's house if you want."

"Are we breaking up?"

"No, not really?"

"What do you mean by not really?"

"I've told you, I have to be in Israel for a while."

"I've got that, but are you kicking me out of this house? Why do you want me to move to my mother's place? I want to stay in my home."

"My family wants to renovate the house, Kate, so it would be better if you stayed some other place. You know you are not on good terms with them."

Kate closed the magazine as he had taken the wind out of her sails. She loved her mother, but she wanted to be the one who chose where she would go and when.

FIFTIETH SCENE

"You told me that I could get anything and you wouldn't interfere with the home decoration."

"Don't get me wrong, it's not me. When I told my family I would be away, they told me they would renovate the house. I can never tell them no, you know that."

"You say no to me—not to them, to me. Okay."

She threw the magazine on the sofa and ran to her room. She slammed the door and lay down on the bed, already regretting what she had done.

*

Kate made a bun of her long blond hair. She looked a lot younger in her yellow shirt, light blue pants and pink sneakers. She was watching herself in a showcase glass, examining herself longer when there were mannequins in the window and checking herself against every woman she thought to be beautiful. She'd had her morning coffee then rushed to the jewelry store that had called the night before. When the door opened, the Indian guy with handlebar mustache smiled.

"Welcome, madam! The collection designed for special customers has arrived, and we called you first."

The guy looked like a penguin in his suit. Kate tried not to laugh.

After a while she remembered she had to visit her mom so she had decided to get a diamond necklace.

"I need to go now. You'll send the necklace to my home?"

"Madam, Rannan Mendel told us the company wouldn't pay us anymore. You have to make the payment."

Kate was too surprised to speak. She had been buying things from this store for years without paying anything.

"Okay."

She gave him her credit card, not even asking the price.

"I'm sorry, madam, this card is invalid."

"How come? Try this one."

"No, madam. The price is higher than your limit."

"How much is that necklace?"

"Seventy-five thousand dollars."

"Okay, I'll buy it later then. Good afternoon."

Kate tried hard not to cry, biting her lip. She was so used to getting what she wanted that she didn't understand what was happening. She sent a message to Rannan.

I was about to buy a necklace from Dream Jewelry but the penguin told me the company has stopped payments. My credit card limit wasn't enough. I feel very bad.

A reply came back:

My family took control of the company. FYI they'll cancel your credit card soon.

Kate was underwater, trying to save her life. Her baby had got lost; the police were looking for him. She woke up immediately. The nightmare had made her feel worse, and she didn't want to think about how real life would make her feel. She was a prisoner in that white house. She had voluntarily locked the doors and swallowed the keys.

She had been home for years, but had never known the house.

FIFTY-FIRST SCENE

Lara followed the crowd and found herself in front of a big stone building. It was the prison on Alcatraz. She entered the building but found it hard to move. People were posing for cameras, smiling. She found it strange to put happy memories on the sorrows of the past. She wanted to have sweet memories on this island with the tourists, but many people had lived here in sorrow and paid the price.

Did having a prison on water have any connection with its cleansing effect? She had a lot of questions yet not many answers. She was walking down a corridor with cells on both sides, feeling cold and hugging herself. Lately she had started internalizing everything. She had spent many days sympathizing with the homeless and now she was trying to do the same thing with the prisoners of Alcatraz. She held the bars and looked inside a cell, putting herself in a prisoner's shoes. She felt like she was looking outside though. It wasn't a joke.

Lara had arrived in America at the end of December. When she first came, she was busy with registration and settling down. That was the reason she didn't know much about December in San Francisco. The end of a year was her beginning, the month that had separated her from her country. She began questioning everything in this new country. She judged herself a lot and sometimes was very cruel and sent herself to prison without batting an eye.

★

It was already evening when Lara finally got back to land and walked to Pier 39. There was an acrobatics show on the street. What she found most interesting was the people standing still, their bodies frozen in a pose. The passers by took photos and then put money into the boxes in front of them.

Lara heard a guitar and followed the music. She knew that white baseball cap and her heart began beating fast. When Johnson finished the song she applauded till her hands got red. Nobody knew that she was really applauding his speech at the university.

Johnson said "Hey" as if he didn't know her. Lara was upset, but she hid it even from herself.

While gathering up the money in his guitar box, Johnson realized there was a hundred dollar bill and gave it back to Lara without a word. Lara took the money without any objection. He was surely a strange man.

Johnson called Joe and they became walking. Lara followed them.

"I'm hungry," said Johnson suddenly. Lara was surprised and smiled at him. They went to Boudin; Lara ordered tomato soup while Johnson ordered crab soup.

Two strangers, sitting together and eating.

"I had this soup when I first came to San Francisco. I found it very interesting as it is in a bread bowl. I like bread, by the way."

Johnson smiled at her.

"Why are you smiling?"

"There is some soup on your mouth."

"Is there still?"

"Well, on your jaw too." He reached out and touched her jaw. Lara blushed and froze.

Johnson finished his soup and crumbled the bread into pieces.

"Joe eats it."

"I don't know where to look for you."

"Look for me on the streets."

Johnson was a talkative and warm man. Lara found it hard to believe he was the same guy who had talked to her class. She laughed with him; it had been quite some time since she had laughed like that. Boudin became her new Çamlıca hill and the homeless guy became Taner, but she didn't know whether she would fall in love again. Was it possible to love that much again? Taner had been an impossible love, and Lara had never been able to find a love that was possible.

They went to the coast and sat on a bench. The view was as blue as Johnson's eyes.

"I went to Alcatraz today and felt like I was in prison."

Johnson began speaking like he hadn't heard Lara.

"You can't escape from the sounds on the street. The hardest part is when you try to sleep. You lay down on cold, hard ground, but it is the sounds that sting your heart. You get lost in them: the sound of horns, the howling of dogs, the rumbling of your stomach, the croak of crows and the sound of loneliness make it silent in a crowd. You can't warn the guy on the bench for snoring or ask who turned off the lights because you want to read. Nothing is the same on the streets."

Lara's face was blank like she'd lost all her emotions and gestures. She saw the man sleeping on a stone bed, under air blankets, between newspapers, and he was doing it willingly.

"You are on the line between life and death. You drew it yourself."

Lara was learning where she was in her life from a homeless man. While talking to him, she felt both scared and close him. She didn't realize she had put her head on his shoulder at sunset. Johnson didn't know he was holding the hand of the beautiful girl he had seen before. The frog had already turned into prince.

FIFTY-SECOND SCENE

San Francisco was no longer a rascal with low cut pants and hip-hop hat; instead, she dressed for a wedding. The weather was soft as a baby's skin and the weekend air was full of peace.

Meltem was preparing salad. Nuray was rolling meatballs and giving them Şahin to grill. Cihan was playing with Emir on his phone, turning his back on Golden Gate.

Nuray was complaining to Meltem about Lara. Meltem had insisted on her coming to the picnic.

"She isn't here, but meatballs should be eaten hot."

"Mom, look! She is coming with someone. Who is it?" Meltem opened her eyes and mouth wide. "Is he her boyfriend?"

"Shhh. It's none of our business."

Lara was walking toward them in a black tracksuit, white hat and sneakers. She was holding someone's hand.

"Hi, everybody, this is Johnson. We got engaged yesterday. We haven't told anyone yet, you are the first ones to hear the news."

Johnson went toward Cihan and Emir.

"Hi! I've played that game a lot. How many points have you got?"

"A hundred and seven billion, you?"

Lara hugged Johnson's waist from behind.

"Hey, have you met?"

"Welcome, Lara, is he your friend?"

"My fiancé, and my partner in life soon."

Cihan didn't know what to say, so he held out his hand to the African-American man. They shook hands even though Cihan didn't want to.

"Congrats." He was scratching his hand when he put it back in his pocket. "I didn't know."

Johnson held Lara's hand and they looked at each other.

"Thanks, everything happened so fast. We're also very surprised."

The view behind them was like decor for a wedding photoshoot. Cihan imagined them in their wedding finery.

"Aunt Nuray, we'll have a quick walk around before dinner. When will it be ready?"

Şahin held up all his fingers. Ten minutes.

"By the way, congrats, Lara, on your engagement."

"Thanks a lot, Uncle Şahin, I'm very happy."

When they left, Nuray began talking as she was preparing the last meatballs.

"Who is this guy? Does Lara's mother know? I haven't asked that—I will when they come back."

Cihan sat down to calm down. He wasn't in love with Lara, but the news hurt him nonetheless. Edom and he were about to break up and he was hoping to start something with Lara. He hadn't given her any idea, but he had planned everything and now all his plans had collapsed because of that blue-eyed man.

*

FIFTY-SECOND SCENE

Cihan left his car with his father and walked around the city all day. It was near midnight when he took a taxi home, and he was unable to tell the driver the way.

"To the left or the right, sir?"

Cihan was very confused in the city he had lived in for years.

"Actually I live in a very easy to find place, but you haven't been able to find it. Strange."

"Are you drunk, sir? I've been following your directions. You must have forgotten the way to your home. How come you don't know the name of the street you live on?"

The taxi driver stopped and left him on Union Square.

"I'll leave you near the homeless, sir. Remember your way home then take a taxi. I don't want your money."

Cihan walked down the street slowly. Who could he ask to help him find his way home?

FIFTY-THIRD SCENE

Meltem leaned on the tall column of a bank on Van Ness. Running down the street as fast as time, she was hitting a wall. She was already thin, but because of the drugs she was so thin that she was almost invisible in her blue flowery dress.

It had been easy for Meltem to say, "This body is mine. I'll take whatever I want." Nobody liked her; Lara was getting married and Nicole had become a mother, but she was always lonely. Her family was only interested in her school success. She had entered a university they liked, but she was still an addict. Her ambition for success had given her the addiction as a present.

She hid her breaths in small orange capsules. She wanted to take them all and be able to breathe again. Her mind was already lost, but her body still wanted more. Meltem was shivering under a thick blanket yet was also on fire. What was the point of staying? Nobody cared about her while she was hurtling toward death at full speed. Her body had no objections. She could leave and the ones she left behind would have no regrets.

"This body is yours, so you can use it however you like. Then stop these voices, the cells dying and your state of mind. Come at your feelings and shut your conscience up, if you really are the owner of your body."

FIFTY-FOURTH SCENE

A mother and daughter were walking in front of Reb. The little girl must have been the same age as Mariana and had tied her black hair just like her. When her ice-cream fell down on the ground, she began crying and her mother hugged her. Reb felt very bad and thought of Mariana. The next thing she did was to get on the bus and go directly to Umah's home. She had finally lost all the will to stay away from that home.

*

Umah's home and the ones in it were foreign to Reb. She didn't want to be a burden to them anymore. Being a guest was trying; she could get tired of compliments and having her laundry done, cooked meals and money in her pocket.

Umah was preparing lunch in the kitchen. Reb was watching Mirza and Mariana playing with the button of the lamp, then suddenly it came on. Everybody looked at her; she had been caught.

When Mirza left her in the room with Mariana, she grabbed her hands. The warmth that filled her inside her was much more beautiful than the warmth caused by smoking and drinking on the coldest of nights. The love of a mother for her child was the sweetest fire.

Reb was tidying herself up, putting her hand on her ear then touching her bangs. Still she wasn't able to escape from worrying about how she would look to a man. At the same time Mariana was listening to her favorite fairytale on her mother's knees.

"Mom, why are you still wearing your jacket? I don't like it at all. Take it off! Are you going to leave again?"

"No, I am not going anywhere, dear. Don't worry."

"Mom?"

"Yes, my dear."

"Are we still homeless?"

"What are you talking about, Mariana? Being homeless means being without a roof. Look up!"

"Yes, we have a roof. Yay, here is our home!"

"Actually, not really."

"So where is?"

"I don't know."

Reb was scared of being without a roof again. What if the streets took her? She closed the curtains of her desires; she was trying to escape from the sun because it might turn dark again.

*

Mirza was wearing a white shirt and black and gray striped pants. He hadn't looked in the mirror for months and his sorrow showed on his face. Today was different, though. He had shaved, combed his hair and put on aftershave, then he looked at himself in the mirror for a long time.

Mirza had promised to take Mariana to the park. Mariana and Reb were waiting for him at the door. Mirza parked his wheelchair in the living room and called his driver. The door opened and Mir-

FIFTY-FOURTH SCENE

za and Reb caught each other's eyes for the first time in months. Mirza blushed, but the heat of his blush was only a little part of his fire.

Mariana hugged Bo and held her mother's hand. She had put her hair in a ponytail with strawberry hairpins and was wearing a pink flowery dress Umah had bought for her. Reb was wearing a red jumper, black pants and a long black jacket. She had a matching hat on her head. All her clothes were presents from Sadaf.

Mirza waited for them to walk to the car, saying, "Ladies first!"

It was rainy in San Francisco so the traffic was slow.

"Mom, look! The sky's ice is melting so its drops are falling to the ground like a kid is crying in the sky."

"How do you know that? Who told you?"

Mirza entered the conversation.

"You haven't forgotten then? You are an awesome, sweet girl."

"Of course I haven't, because it was me. I was crying over my mom leaving, remember? It was raining on that day too. You told me the clouds were crying with me, and if I cried a lot we'd be under water. I stopped crying because of that."

Reb's blood drained from her face; her mouth got dry. What she had heard had opened a closed wound, and it was bleeding again.

"My dear, it is all over. I will never leave you again."

She hugged Mariana and kissed her head.

The car stopped and the driver helped Mirza to get out and sit in his wheelchair. Reb and Mariana also got out of the car. The rain had stopped. Reb pushed Mirza into the park; Mirza put his hand on Reb's to thank her.

"I should thank you. You've opened your home for us."

After a short walk they sat on a bench. After a while a small dog with brown fur came over and Mariana asked permission to pet him. The owner of the dog was a white haired old man who was happy to tell Mariana about the dog.

Mirza glanced at Reb's face. He knew Reb was also looking at him, so he focused on the water. There were boats on the lake, painting their surroundings with peace. Reb was happy sitting beside Mirza, but she was scared of the power of the things he was approaching saying to her.

"Reb, I've been waiting for this moment for a long time. I want tell you something. Please hear me out, okay?"

"I...okay."

"Reb, I want you by my side until I die. I want Mariana to be my daughter. If you want, I'd like to share my life with you. Will you be my wife?"

He opened a box. There was a golden necklace in it.

"I know I am supposed to give you a ring in this situation, but I had no courage to buy one. I would have had to take back the ring if you didn't accept, but the necklace is yours whatever you decide."

Reb closed her mouth and opened her eyes. She had crashed into an iceberg. Time stopped and her breathing became uneven. She wanted to say something but was unable. Mirza was looking at the woman he loved with the necklace in his hand. There were tears on his face.

"Please, take it whatever your answer is."

Mariana was still petting the dog a few meters away. Reb took the necklace and put it on.

"Yes, yes, YES!"

Mirza wished he was able to stand up. He wanted to run and turn somersaults. Instead he squeezed the wheels of his wheelchair until he had calmed down a little bit.

Mariana wondered what was happening and came over to them. Reb bent down beside Mariana and looked into her eyes, taking her warm hands.

"My dear, I've accepted Mirza's proposal before checking it's okay with you, but I'm asking you now. If you don't want me to, please tell me."

"What proposal? I like your necklace, who bought it?"

"We have decided to get married, Mirza and me. What do you say?"

Mariana stopped for a moment, pretending to be thinking to get the two of them agitated.

"Okay, but you'll have to let me wear the necklace from time to time."

Reb was crying. She wouldn't have to long for that warm home of her dreams anymore. She didn't care that the man she loved was in a wheelchair and from another religion and culture. The only thing she knew was someone was in love with her. Reb opened the black curtains inside herself. The sun shone in and made reflections on her home necklace.

FIFTY-FIFTH SCENE

After the marriage ceremony in the church, Lara and Johnson went to a restaurant in Ghirardelli with close friends. The black jeep stopped and Johnson opened the back door.

Lara got out of the car, holding the train of her long white dress. She had left her hair untied and wore a little makeup. Johnson looked a different person in his white suit; Lara loved white most on Johnson. Lara and Johnson climbed the stairs arm in arm, followed by Sadaf, Cihan, Nuray, Emir, Meltem, Mirza and Reb.

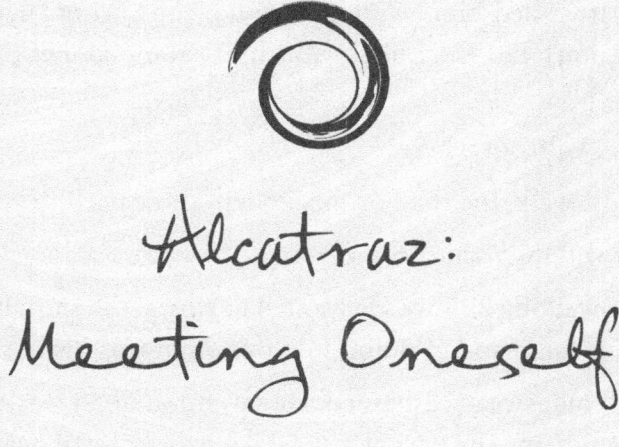

Alcatraz: Meeting Oneself

Cihan was going to a meeting with his own reality. He was in a hurry and anxious. He had given himself a time, facing up to all the time he hadn't given. He didn't know what would have happened to him by the end of the day; all he wanted was the day to end. Every day of his life had ended, so this day would eventually end too. He was accounting for the time he had wasted every other day. He had been waiting for today on the train of missing tomorrows, but all tomorrows become today.

He was going to the place where he would become himself. He was going to meet with his soul as his heart had called him and given him one last chance.

"You have to come alone."

His heart had added this as he always brought somebody with him. Arrogance, jealousy, selfishness were all following him. Cihan was also fed up with them, so he would go alone, determined to rescue himself from himself.

Cihan was climbing a hill with a black bag in his hand. In this bag were his loved ones, ones he didn't love, his dreams and his desires.

His heart called him again and said: "Don't bring anyone with you, and don't call the police. You must come alone. Only you. Got it?"

"Okay, I will, but where?"

"You just walk, the road or the sea will show itself to you."

"What will the road show me?"

He was walking blindly. He wanted to stop at the start, but walking held his hand and told him to move on. It was his last chance.

He felt cold, sweaty, ashamed. He sat, stood up. It wasn't easy to become a human. The part of him which was afraid of death wasn't actually scared of his dead parts. He ignored that part. It was like committing a murder. For those who destroyed their souls, death was deserved.

Cihan became more and more human with every step he took inside himself. Instead of becoming many other things, he again became himself. Not a tree, bird, stone or building, simply a human. He should have left his relentlessness long ago; he had been acting without thinking. He was an ordinary man of ordinary things, so he picked up everything he had and walked to become human.

FIFTY-SIXTH SCENE

Cihan hugged his own body like he was hugging a small kitty in the cold. His childish side was shivering in the storm of his soul. He could hear the sound of his organs and it was devastating.

"I'm going to the shore."

Cihan knew Edom would follow him, and actually he dragged him with his body language. He felt the air at home wouldn't be able to handle what he was going to say. He needed an ocean and a sky. He had gotten tired of bad scenes so he wanted to watch the blue.

Cihan felt Edom beside him, but he stood still. He locked his look on the white crests of the waves. If it was possible to drink all the water in the ocean, he might have found himself there. He was becoming less himself again. He felt sorry for himself when he saw the pieces falling from him.

He put his fists on his lap and began talking. His voice was soft, yet his words were very hard.

"Edom, I want to break up. It isn't happening for me, I just can't. You know, it wasn't my choice. I went for it as I couldn't say no to you, because of curiosity, or stupidity. My soul was in the wrong direction. I crashed someplace in my heart. My feelings were cruel, they broke me."

Cihan had never liked talking from heart. It felt as though he was throwing his feelings up. He was gagging to release the grip on his conscience. His words sounded bitter.

"Cihan, I thought you were happy. Everything was fine. It hasn't been a year yet. You should give us a little time. You'll see, everything will be different."

Cihan was hitting the wall. His hair flopped down over his thick eyebrows. He licked his lips and spread his hands.

"She got married."

Edom learned the reason for their separation in that moment. The possibility that had made them come together had been impossible all along.

"I see!" Edom shook his Los Angeles keychain. "But you have no chance of getting her because she is married."

"I know we can't be together, but the news hurt me. I felt like she was my only way out. Anyway, I've made a decision. I want to live in peace from now on. I have no power to cope with the riot in me. What I am sure of is that if I get married one day, it will be to a woman."

"Baby!"

Cihan looked at Edom's face.

"What baby?"

"The baby that represents our lives."

"What's this bullshit? Don't tell me you're pregnant."

"The email that I wrote to you after you left Golden Gate Park. You deleted it without reading it?"

"Yes, I remember. I asked you a couple of times about it but you didn't tell me what it said."

"I wrote *two men can't make a baby*."

FIFTY-SIXTH SCENE

Cihan lowered his voice, shy about the people around hearing.

"What does that mean, Edi?"

"When I was in second grade in junior high, a friend of mine kissed me in the locker room after we'd won a game. I pushed him away and he said, 'You don't have to worry. Two men can't make a baby'. Then one day I heard my mom talking to yours about how she couldn't marry my father because of religion and her life had been ruined because of me. You can't comprehend the pain I felt at that moment. It is very hurtful to realize you are a jail to the woman who gave birth to you. I promised myself that day I would live my life freely and no baby would ever imprison me."

Edom couldn't continue. He felt abandoned in the dark woods; he heard the sounds of the vultures. There was no way forward, but Cihan was running backwards . Even though they had been together physically, Cihan's soul had left. He was running toward the night on the bridge; then his aim had been to return to their childhood.

Edom got in his car and sat inside it for a while, looking like a mannequin on the driver's seat. He started as a car horn sounded.

"Are you leaving, sir?"

"Yes, I am. If only I knew where to go!"

"Excuse me?"

"Nothing. I'm moving."

Edom started the car with the keys on the keychain Cihan had bought for him. He felt like Cihan had given it to him as a leaving gift. It had been only minutes since Cihan had left him, but it felt like years.

A black coat was there on the shore, but it seemed like it was empty. Who would even know their relationship had happened? When you said it was nonexistent, it ceased to be.

⋆

There was the sound of beeps, the smell of drugs, doctors with masks, opening doors and desperate people waiting for the patient to come round. Cihan was one of them. He was restless without understanding the situation.

"Cihan, I'm talking to you, son. Do you hear me?"

Nuray wanted her son to bend down a little so she could whisper in his ear.

"You should gather yourself. People will think you're the husband."

Cihan lost his temper. His mother saw a married woman, a woman in death throes, as a threat to him.

"Okay, Mom. She is in the razor's range, you are talking nonsense."

Cihan put his hand in his pocket and walked down the corridor. Two policemen were trying to get information from Johnson. He was trying to calm his feet by moving them constantly.

"I couldn't stop her. I told her a car was coming, but I couldn't stop her. I told her a car was coming, but I couldn't stop her."

He was in a shock, repeating the same thing again and again.

"I know you're in pain, sir."

Johnson calmed down a little bit.

"When did you marry Lara?"

"Two months ago. Two, two, two."

He was showing two fingers.

"What's your occupation?"

"Me?"

"Of course you."

FIFTY-SIXTH SCENE

"I don't work."

"What is your occupation?"

"My occupation...My occupation...I forgot."

"Okay, sir. Where were you coming from? What were you doing in the airport?"

"We went on honeymoon to Europe. We saw her mother in Turkey, then her grandmother in Munich."

"You have no job but go to Europe on honeymoon. Where did the money for that come from? Strange."

"My wife covered the expenses, she is rich. We shouldn't have gone. Dammit, we shouldn't have gone!"

Johnson began hitting the walls.

"Hey, sir, please calm down."

"Can you describe the car?"

"Lemon, lemon, lemon."

"What do you mean? The color?"

"Yes, yes, yes. It was a roadster sports car, I didn't see the driver. Please, don't die. I have just found my home. If you go, I'll become homeless again."

Cihan held his head as it was spinning. It couldn't be a coincidence, but he didn't want to believe that Edom had got that mad.

"Answer the damn phone, you bastard!"

Edom wasn't answering. Cihan was about to go crazy. He entered the hospital again with someone right behind him.

"Your mother was worried about you so I came here to check," said Sadaf.

"I'm okay."

When he came into the waiting room he asked if there was any news.

"It hasn't been five minutes yet. What news? Where have you been? Sadaf told us you got cold and asked for a jacket."

Sadaf wanted to curl up and die but tried not to look ashamed.

"I'm going then."

"Where are you going, Cihan? Home? Don't go to bed without eating first, promise."

The last thing on Cihan's mind was hunger. Even if he had eaten everything in sight, his soul would still have been hungry.

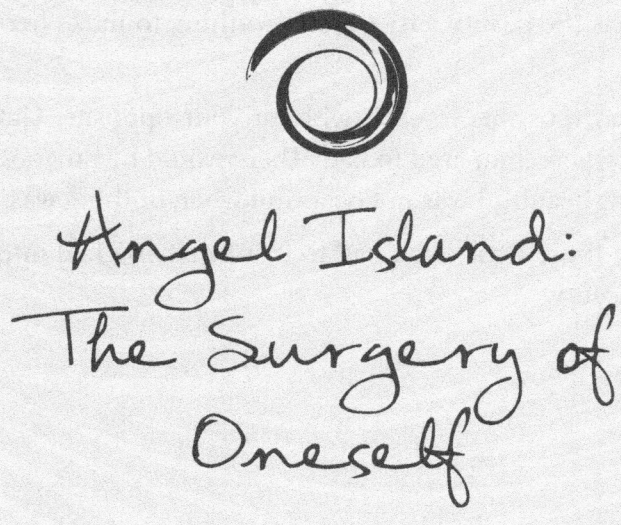

Angel Island: The Surgery of Oneself

Cihan was in the surgery room of the soul as he was planning to cut out everything ugly and bad. He lay himself down on a big stretcher, turning the white lights on to see everything better. He was as hungry as the wolf in the 'Little Red Riding Hood' story. He had to release himself from unreasonable dreams, bad ideas and bad acts, then ultimately he would become an angel.

Cihan lay his body down on the stretcher and scratched his eyes out to stop them from taking a fancy to the beautiful ones. It was time to cut off his ears so as not to hear tempting offers. He then cut out his tongue so as not to say anything bad. After breaking his nose to purify himself from bad smells, he cut his hands so he couldn't press the red button.

The door of the Imperial Suite in his body palace was locked. It was hard to enter his heart. He had pulled everything out and assumed he would be lighter now, but all beauty had left him as it couldn't be seen where there was no ugliness.

Becoming an angel was not possible for a human.

■

"Why has the beauty left? I did everything to make her to stay with me."

It was not possible to exist without your opposite. Good was only good when compared to bad. There would be no good deeds without sin. Beautiful was not beautiful when nothing was ugly.

To open those doors, you had to turn what you had into goodness and beauty.

FIFTY-EIGHTH SCENE

Cihan left Nuray and Meltem at the hospital and came home after midnight having bought something to eat as a result of his mother's insistence. There was a small package on the door knob with no name on it. Cihan opened it. There were two lipsticks inside, one black and one purple, with a note.

I know why you gave these to me, Nuray. Because of the color of the life I'm living, I can't see the sky anymore. I'm very sad. My lover got bored with me and left me for another woman. My husband is happy with his new lover. I feel very defenseless, desperate and lonely. This is not freedom. I want the natural color of my lips, and I want my real self.

The door was banged twice. Cihan turned down the volume of the TV and slowly approached the door. When he opened it, he saw someone's back wearing a green coat, a big flowered hat and red high heels.

"Hello, madam, who are you looking for? I'm afraid you're in the wrong place."

He waited for her to turn round, and when she didn't he closed the door. He could feel she was still there, so he turned up the volume so high that he couldn't hear the door.

She kept knocking.

"What do you want? Who are you?" Cihan yelled at her from the sofa, hiding behind his voice to prove he wasn't afraid. When he finally opened the door he had to cover his mouth with his hands.

"*You?*"

"Yes, me."

She walked into the middle of the living room. It was the first time Edom had walked with her shoes in Cihan's house.

"Well, it's me. You don't have to wait anymore, Cihan. Lara is in vegetative state, she will die soon. You wanted to be with a woman, I'm ready to start all over."

She slowly took off her gloves and hat and shook her long blond wig.

"Do you like my new hair, my dress? These are all for you."

Chan was standing beside the door without knowing what to say or do. Edom was there as a woman.

"Don't worry, darling, I have already pushed the car into the ocean. I'm a woman now."

She was circling Cihan, hitting her gloves against her palm. She leaned close to Cihan's ear and whispered, "Don't call me Edom. Call me Ece."

"Ece? Where did you come up with that name?"

"Ece, a Turkish name. Look, I have more pluses than minuses. Can you still resist me?"

Cihan opened the door and checked the surroundings.

"Did anyone follow you? Go away now or I'll..."

He raised his hand to slap Edom.

"You can't do that!"

"Of course I can!"

"If you report me, you'll regret it."

FIFTY-EIGHTH SCENE

Cihan was afraid of Edom for the first time in his life.

When there were no boundaries, you couldn't put an end to something. Desire was sometimes hell; you would understand that if you followed it. The last stop was fire. Cihan was sure now that Edom had run into Lara. Not knowing was best sometimes. What was he to do with this information? He didn't know what caused the most sorrow: a woman was about to die because of him, the murderer in a woman's body was asking him to escape with him or the person who had caused all of this was his best friend. It was surely a dark night.

Cihan was neither out nor in the house. Edom was lost in the dark like a shadow. He knew the sun wouldn't visit him anymore. There was no escape for him. Cihan felt like he was the one to blame; he had given himself to his curiosity. Lara was only an excuse to leave; she shouldn't have been the one who paid the price.

Cihan was willing to live as if at the North Pole with six months of day and six of night, but now he only had night. His conscience was hurting him; how could he live without a roof over his head?

FIFTY-NINTH SCENE

Rannan Mendel was at the police station getting information on the incident. Kate was waiting on a chair silently. She was there in name only; her real desire was to die. With every breath she took she longed for death as Edom would be charged with murder if Lara died.

Rannan was walking up and down with a phone in his hand, shouting.

"How come? That's ridiculous! It was an accident, officer, please bail him out."

The policemen were trying to get him to sit.

"No way, sir."

"Can you please tell me when he will be released?"

"Look, we have no idea. We are investigating the incident, but I'm afraid nobody believes it was an accident. We have evidence he intended to kill her. He might have had a relationship with the girl he ran into."

"Impossible, he is a homosexual."

"Yes, it's a little complicated, but it's not a simple crime. If the girl dies, your son will…"

A scream rang out at that moment. Kate was in such pain that she had to let it out. She couldn't believe her son was capable of killing someone.

FIFTY-NINTH SCENE

"You have to leave now, sir, and tell your wife to stay indoors for her own sake."

Rannan caught Kate's eyes as she stood beside the door.

"Kate, what do you think you're doing?"

Kate had fallen down and was hugging Rannan's knees.

"Do something, Rannan, do something! Get my son out of jail, I'm begging you!"

"He is also my son, Kate, calm down please!"

"He is not a bad person. He doesn't commit crimes; tell me he didn't do it. Please. It was an accident!"

Kate lost all connection with life when she heard her son was going to prison. She was among the living-dead now.

SIXTIETH SCENE

Sadaf and Cihan were sitting on a bench in the hospital garden. Sadaf was squinting as she had left her sunglasses in the car. She was wearing her white scarf, black turtleneck sweater and no makeup. Cihan took off his leather jacket and put it on his knees. He hadn't shaved for a while so he was shaggy. Sadaf didn't dare tell him, but she liked this look on him.

She took a sip from her coffee.

"Don't blame yourself, Cihan, you didn't do anything wrong. Lara would say the same thing and be hurt to see you so sad."

"Thanks, Sadaf. Do you know you sweeten me up? I feel relaxed listening to you."

Sadaf blushed with happiness. She met him three times a week in the hospital garden; Cihan was deep in regret and Sadaf was trying to make him feel better. Cihan had put himself entirely in her hands. He was ready to surrender to a woman who would be a safe harbor for him. Sadaf seemed like the one, yet he still didn't feel anything for her.

"Let's put the flowers in her room."

"They are not for Lara, they are yours."

"Mine?"

Cihan gave the flowers to Sadaf. The floor gave way and the curtains of the sky opened. Tears of happiness ran down her cheeks,

SIXTIETH SCENE

but she would say it was because of the rain. Sadaf knew that when a woman got flowers from the man she loved, the clouds would cry. The clouds were applauding with rain and the ones under them got soaked with love.

SIXTY-FIRST SCENE

Rannan Mandel stuck his fork into an omelet during breakfast, but he didn't eat any. He was about to take a bite from a sausage, then stopped.

"Did you prepare breakfast?"

"Yes, a little surprise for you. Maya is taking time off. Do you like it?"

"Why didn't you consult me?"

"How could I ask about a surprise?"

"Kate, I have never complained about you taking cookery classes and trying things out in the kitchen, yet you still have no idea about kosher rules!"

"Kosher rules?"

"If you cook dairy and meat in the same place, it isn't kosher for Jews. Why do you think we have two fridges, ovens and washing machines?"

"For lots of guests? I'm so sorry."

"Okay, no worries. I have news for you. The lawyer told me that Edom is coming out tomorrow, but he can't come here as I lost all my money bailing him out."

"I'll leave, then."

SIXTY-FIRST SCENE

Kate went to her room and packed her things up, smiling while randomly filling her case. She wasn't leaving home, she was going home. The white mansion had never been her home.

Edom's getting out of prison became her getting out of prison. There was only one night between them and freedom.

★

The doors opened. The sun blinded his eyes. A woman was looking at the man who had just stepped outside. Edom had changed a lot: his baby face had become more mature with red spots on it.

Kate and Edom hugged each other and stood without talking for a while.

"I've left home, Edom. I don't know if the lawyer told you, but Rannan sold your apartment to bail you out and told me he would not give you anything."

"It's okay, Mom. I don't want anything from him."

"What are you going to do now?"

"I don't know. I'll figure something out."

"I'm going to your grandma's home, you could come with me."

"No, Mom. I'd like to be alone for a while. Don't worry about me."

Kate watched her son take a taxi after hugging her.

"From now on everything will be better."

SIXTY-SECOND SCENE

Nuray was putting the dishes in the dishwasher. She put the glasses in and tried to close the door, but she wasn't able to. Something must have been stacked wrongly. She searched for the problem, moved the dishes around, even forced it to close, but she wasn't successful.

She began crying, not because of the dishwasher, but because she needed to clean her dreams and made her hopes shiny again. She let her tears drop, then looked at the dishwasher again calmly and suddenly realized the problem. A fork was stuck in the door. She had never checked there. It was the final straw.

Nuray no longer waited for her husband to come to her. She was proud of herself as she wiped the possibilities out. Yet sometimes, when she saw old couples walking on the seashore, she hurt. It was hard getting used to being away from her children.

*

Meltem was often alone in the green house on Turk Street in San Francisco. Her father went on business trips a lot and Cihan was living in San Diego with his wife, Sadaf.

"Meltem, how are you? How are your studies going? You are coming to Istanbul when school is finished, right?"

"School is fine, Mom. When it is finished, I will stay here. What would I do in Turkey?"

"You would do what I'm doing, dear: work."

"Nope, Mom. I'm thinking about visiting you for two weeks, but I'm not gonna stay any longer."

Nuray never insisted on her staying in Turkey after that talk. She wanted everyone to live where they were happy. Nuray was happy as Meltem was clean from drugs. It was okay for her to be far away as long as she was healthy.

SIXTY-THIRD SCENE

Johnson was following a heart monitor with his eyes. When the line dropped, Johnson felt like he was falling down a hill, and when the opposite happened he felt like he was flying. The heart was beating so life was still there and death could wait.

A man approached Johnson and put a hand on his shoulders. He said, "One million dollars have been put into Lara's account. I know it is your joint account. Nothing will bring her health back, but at least take this money as a consolation."

"I know this is not a consolation, sir. Rannan Mandel sent this money to shut me up so the reputation of Mandel Chocolate Factory will be safe. Don't worry, sir, your money will be donated to charity."

The line became flat so the life left. A man screamed beside a hospital bed.

"Noooooo!"

The home collapsed.

Homeless was homeless again.

Treasure Island: Space

Lara would build a spaceship to go up into her soul's space, but she had to find out what she needed first. She had to find very powerful dynamite for a strong liftoff. She needed to have enough food so she wouldn't starve in space. Memorizing the buttons on the spaceship was essential. The clothes she would wear and the flow of the time would change and her feelings would disappear, but she would get used to it. There was no other way she could get to know herself.

She had finished building the spaceship after ten years and finally it was time to take off. She checked everything and took up a fetal position. She was innocent and pure like a baby. Going up into soul space was hard but also peaceful. She was watching her world from her heart's eye. The people in soul space were floating in the world of meaning.

Lara had to search soul space to meet herself because she was much more than the body she had seen in the mirror. She shot herself into soul space; she had to travel there to find new lands.

Everything was different in soul space. Being there meant standing on the line between existence and nonexistence. Wearing special clothes, she was gathering data to work on her truth.

There were islands in soul space. She chose Treasure Island so she could reach her inside treasure and bring it to the truth.

Return and After

Lara was feeling as light as a feather. She was sick, vomiting and having headaches. Her whole body was trying to keep up with the changes caused by the return.

She wasn't able to estimate the weight of objects. It was possible that she was mentally unstable. She also had depression and anxiety problems. When hormones changed and mobility was limited, hyperkinesia occurred. There were different drugs in space. The need to sleep and the lack of senses were only a couple of the changes.

She didn't take off her space clothes for a while after her return. It was taking time for her skin to adapt to the changes, just like it would for humans.

She was on earth, playing in hot lava. The earth was always earth as she was always the sky.

SIXTY-FOURTH SCENE

His ripped blue jeans were too large for him so his black boxers were visible. The pocket of his navy-blue velvet jacket was bouncing on his hip. He had put his head in the garbage, looking for food, when he heard brakes squeal followed by a horn. An African-American man in a gray suit and sunglasses gave him a pizza box. The homeless man was very surprised and made some wild noises.

Before taking the pizza, the homeless man spat in his hands and wiped them on his clothes. Shaking his head, he said, "Thank you, sir, God bless you." Then, without wasting any more time, he grabbed the box and sat on the ground.

Johnson never found out he had just helped his wife's murderer. Edom was also unaware Johnson was Lara's husband.

Before the car moved away, the African-American man saw an overthrown trolley on the grass and some bottles on the road. The sunlight was reflecting off them. The reflections were as attractive as the world, but fragile and temporary as the ones in it. He looked for an eternal light, but was unable to find one because he was lifeless anyway.

Cihan, Meltem, Lara and Sadaf watched the big screen with surprise. They had just watched the movie of their lives. They were already in another world.

At the last stop on the one way road, they asked whoever was listening: "Was it me doing all of that?"

*

The three islands in San Francisco—Alcatraz, Treasure Island and Angel Island—represent the places where humans go according to the things they pass through.

Johnson is the state of homelessness.

Home represents a shelter, a roof, peace and happiness.

Recognizing Him means having a home; denying Him means being homeless.

CONTENTS

First Scene 3
Second Scene 19
Third Scene. 23
Islands *30*
Treasure Island: The Machine of States *31*
Fourth Scene 33
Alcatraz: Garbage *40*
Treasure Island: The Aspects of Feelings *43*
Sixth Scene (Sunday 6.45 p.m.) 44
Treasure Island: The Season of the Heart *46*
Seventh Scene 48
Eighth Scene 51
Ninth Scene 53
Tenth Scene 56
Alcatraz: Heart-The Boss *59*
Eleventh Scene 61
Twelfth Scene 67
Thirteenth Scene 72
Alcatraz: Loneliness *76*

Fourteenth Scene	78
Alcatraz: The Rain Curtain	*83*
Fifteenth Scene	84
Sixteenth Scene	89
Seventeenth Scene	91
Eighteenth Scene	95
Nineteenth Scene	101
Twentieth Scene	107
Twenty-first Scene	111
Twenty-second Scene	115
Angel Island: The Building of the Heart's Eye	*120*
Twenty-third Scene	122
Twenty-fourth Scene	128
Alcatraz: The Ear Window	*132*
Twenty-fifth Scene	133
Twenty-sixth Scene	139
Alcatraz: The Knife	*143*
Twenty-seventh Scene	144
Twenty-eighth Scene	146
Treasure Island: Bridge	*148*
Twenty-ninth Scene	149
Alcatraz: Telephone	*151*
Thirtieth Scene	152
Alcatraz: Riot	*155*
Thirty-first Scene	156
Thirty-second Scene	159

Thirty-third Scene	164
Thirty-fourth Scene	167
Thirty-fifth Scene	171
Thirty-sixth Scene	174
Thirty-seventh Scene	175
Thirty-eighth Scene	178
Thirty-ninth Scene	180
Alcatraz: The White Shirt with Five Holes	*184*
Fortieth Scene	185
Forty-first Scene	189
Alcatraz: Bicycle	*190*
Forty-second Scene	191
Forty-third Scene	194
Forty-fourth Scene	198
Alcatraz: Upside-down World	*203*
Forty-fifth Scene	204
Forty-sixth Scene	208
Forty-seventh Scene	213
Forty-eighth Scene	214
Forty-ninth Scene	217
Fiftieth Scene	219
Fifty-first Scene	223
Fifty-second Scene	227
Fifty-third Scene	230
Fifty-fourth Scene	231
Fifty-fifth Scene	236

Alcatraz: Meeting Oneself. *237*
Fifty-sixth Scene 239
Angel Island: The Surgery of Oneself. *245*
Fifty-eighth Scene 247
Fifty-ninth Scene. 250
Sixtieth Scene. 252
Sixty-first Scene 254
Sixty-second Scene 256
Sixty-third Scene 258
Treasure Island: Space *259*
Return and After. *260*
Sixty-fourth Scene. 261
About the Author 267

ABOUT THE AUTHOR

Zeynep Guvenc is a freelance writer and a blogger. She holds a Master of Arts degree in history from Istanbul University, Turkey. She currently lives in Florida with her husband and two kids, and she lived in San Francisco Bay Area for six years prior to that. Zeynep researches extensively about the problems and challenges of youth, homeless people, religion, and different cultures. She worked as a columnist for two different Turkish newspapers. She maintains two blogs, and she is a member of the Young Adult Fiction book group in Florida.

Made in the USA
Las Vegas, NV
26 September 2021